CYRUS

SMOKEJUMPERS

BOOK TWO

BY EVIE RILEY

Cyrus

Smokejumpers

Book Two

Copyright © 2023

Evie Riley

Second Edition

ISBN: 978-1-77357-680-0

Published by Naughty Nights Press LLC

Cover Art By Willsin Rowe

CYRUS

A sexy fireman. One smokin' hot hookup. Sparks of passion ignite...

Four generations of firefighters in his family make Captain Damon Amaro a legacy member—a prestigious status handed down to him only because of his name. A legacy he'd rather he didn't have, but familial obligations have always been his downfall.
Struggling with the fact that his older brother is currently on trial for multiple arson and murder charges, Damon turns to less-than-savory extracurricular activities to help him cope. Even his best friend has no idea about the secrets he's been hiding.

After changing his name to escape the shame of his father's misdeeds, Cyrus MacMillan is the newest firefighter at Station Twenty-One. He joined the fire department in an attempt to right the cosmic wrongs his father committed, and now he just hopes that information stays buried.

Trust is a difficult thing for Cyrus, so when Damon and he connect on a level beyond his wildest dreams, he knows it probably won't last long. Especially when his past is suddenly made public.

Damon believes the sins of the father should never be cast on the son, and he supports Cy in his goals, even if it means keeping their budding relationship on the down-low while Cy finishes his rookie days at the firehouse. Both men have baggage they have to overcome, but in the end, they believe they are better together.

Can Damon and Cy have a future together, or will continuing their relationship have repercussions neither of them can live with?

CHAPTER ONE

Damon

THE LITTLE LIGHT changed from red to green and I strolled into the hotel room. This wasn't the first time I'd done this in the past three months. It wasn't even the tenth. I wasn't one for one-night stands. I didn't tend to do this. There was too much risk involved.

As a Captain in the Investigations

Unit of the Fire Department, I was supposed to live up to a level of reputation and ethics. I couldn't have questionable morals or make questionable decisions, and up until three months ago I never had.

Up until three months ago, I'd always made sure that none of my actions would be questionable. I never got drunk on a weekday. Hell, I'd never gotten drunk on weekends. I'd never smoked, done drugs, or engaged in reckless sex. I'd never allowed myself to take risks, to ever be in a compromising position.

The past three months, though, I'd been reckless. I'd been spiraling and I knew I shouldn't be, but it was hard to stop now. I'd been getting drunk multiple times a week, even on weekdays. I'd gone to sex parties, actual sex parties in an underground secret club with drugs. I'd done ecstasy and cocaine, something I never thought I would do, but I did them. I enjoyed doing them. It was wrong and I shouldn't have done it, but I couldn't seem to stop.

It was as if I had spent my whole life living in a box and having to do everything perfect, everything right. And for the first time in thirty-eight years, I'd broken out of that box and now I was struggling to get back inside.

The trick was, I didn't know if I truly wanted to go back inside that box. My whole life I'd had to be perfect. I'd had to uphold the reputation of my family, my family name, multiple generations of firefighters.

People often thought being a legacy meant we had it easier. That we got instant respect and had a golden road paved ahead of us. What they didn't realize is that everyone looked at us like we were supposed to be amazing. Like we came into the world capable of extinguishing the most deadly of fires without breaking a sweat. The reality was, though, that wasn't me.

I'd never wanted to be a firefighter. I'd never had any interest in running into a burning building. I'd had a great deal of respect for every firefighter, for every man and woman who were brave and courageous enough to run into an inferno to save lives. But that just wasn't me. It wasn't because I wasn't brave or courageous; it was because I didn't like fire.

I grew up with my father and grandfather both going through horrific days. Days where they drank themselves into oblivion just so they didn't have to deal with the emotions and trauma they felt. I'd watched as my father slowly faded away. As his smile started to appear less and less. As the drinking increased, as the anger increased, as the fighting increased. I'd had a front row seat to all of it, and the very last thing I'd wanted to do was put my future husband or myself in that position.

I can still remember clear as day what my father's face looked like when I told him that I didn't want to sign up for the fire academy. I was seventeen and I thought he would be okay with me not wanting to be a firefighter because my older brother, Taye, was already one.

Taye was older by a few years and he had always wanted to be a firefighter. He had always been interested in fire and he signed up right when he turned eighteen without hesitation. I thought I would be okay to chase after my own dreams. I thought my father would allow me to have my own life.

As it turned out, I was wrong.

To my father, both of his sons had to be in the fire department. Otherwise it would be a disgrace to the family name. I'd never told anyone that I didn't want to be a firefighter, only my father knew. I knew most people would have told me to do whatever I wanted. That I was an adult and my father couldn't force me to join the fire department.

It wasn't that simple, though.

My father had a way of making sure you did whatever he wanted. He never raised a hand to us, but he didn't have to. He knew how to keep us in line, how to pile on the pressure and make clear his disappointment if we didn't do as we were told. After eighteen years of it, I knew the only way I wasn't going into the fire academy would be with his permission.

I was never going to get his permission, so I settled for trying to make a life in the fire department that I could live with. Once I graduated from the academy, I immediately took the route of an officer and became a fire investigator. It kept me out of the burning buildings and I naively believed I would be protected from the horrors that took place every day on this job. I'd thought if I investigated fires to determine what caused them, I wouldn't have to experience the trauma that normal firefighters did when they arrived on scene. I never expected that I would have to see the burnt up bodies, the ones so horribly burned, suffering and fighting for their life in the burn unit. I thought it would be just burned out buildings.

I was so very wrong.

Still, I'd dealt with it like I was supposed to. I buried it and pushed through the trauma and pain to do my job. I had a reputation to live up to and that meant I couldn't show any weakness. I had to be perfect and work my way up through the ranks. Now twenty years later, I was a Captain in the Investigation Unit and I was responsible for three dozen men and women with hundreds of open cases.

I had a lot to lose. I had a lot of

reasons why I needed to go back into my perfectly created box. I knew logically I needed to get myself back into that box so I wouldn't drag my family's name and reputation through the mud more than it already had been.

I had always been responsible. I had always been the dependable one. The one who made sure our family name was kept in good standing. And then three months ago one of my best investigators blew up my world.

Tristan Cole had been one of my best guys and I relied on him and his instincts to help close some of the most difficult cases. On top of that, he had an amazing conviction rating. The evidence he found was always exactly what our Assistant District Attorney needed to convince a jury that we had our arsonist. He was a huge asset to the department and I often relied on him to work cases that were left cold.

I just never expected him to change everything in one single shot.

Three months ago, Tristan informed me that my older brother was a suspected arsonist. I didn't want to believe it at first, but it got increasingly hard to ignore all of the signs from growing up and the damming evidence.

Tristan had been working on cold cases since the first day he'd started in the unit. I knew he had been trying to find the arsonist who had started the fire in his family home that killed his parents and left his arm severely burned.

To be honest, I never expected for him to find his arsonist. I had hoped he would, for his own sake, of course, so he could heal and recover from the tragedy. I just never expected for him to discover multiple fires all connected to not one, but two arsonists. I thought he was crazy. I told him as much. I thought he was trying to see a pattern where there wasn't one, only for him to have been right the whole time.

I should have listened to him years ago. Maybe if I had, Taye wouldn't have had the chance to kill anyone yet. But I didn't listen and fifteen years had gone by with Taye and his mentor setting fires and killing people. Taye himself had been starting fires for ten years, ever since our father had been killed in a storage facility fire.

I still wasn't certain Taye hadn't started that fire.

I knew he wouldn't have wanted to kill our father, but he wouldn't have known that would have been the result. I had asked Tristan to look into it, but so far he hadn't been able to find anything definitive.

Taye was now in prison awaiting trial for multiple homicides, including two young children. His mentor, Wilson Stan, was dead, killed by Taye himself when their relationship reached its boiling point.

I knew from my career that arsonists didn't usually work in pairs. It was very rare for an arsonist to want to work with someone, to teach someone his hands on methods, and I suspected that Wilson had a more complex psyche than the average arsonist. Unfortunately, we would never truly know now that he was dead.

What it did mean was that for the past ten years every fire that we could connect to Wilson or Taye, Taye could be charged with the fire and any injuries or deaths associated with it. It didn't matter if Taye lit the fuse, all that mattered legally was that it could be connected to any fire that Taye had been part of.

So far, Taye was refusing to speak to anyone, he wasn't going to confess, so it was up to Assistant District Attorney Barba to get a conviction. I knew he would, though. He might not get a conviction on every fire, but he would on the murder of Wilson Stan and the attempted murder of Detective West and Tristan. Both Detective West and Tristan had survived the nightmare and they were both set to testify. Taye would be going to prison for the rest of his life.

Along with my family's name and legacy.

A knock at my door dragged me out of my thoughts. Tonight I was meeting up with a guy that I'd messaged on Grinder named Cy. That was all his profile had for a name, along with a very nice picture of his bare chest and a sexy face. He was younger, but I didn't care. I wasn't looking to date or marry anyone. This was just about having some fun, hooking up and letting off some steam.

Cy's profile didn't reveal anything about him personally. I had no idea what his job was or if he went to school or not. I didn't care about any of that shit anyway, and the profiles that came across as someone looking for something more or ongoing, I skipped over them.

Nope. Not my deal.

I strolled over and opened the door and was instantly relieved to see that he matched his profile picture. There had been a couple of times where a profile picture wasn't exactly a match to what the hookup looked like in person. They weren't a completely different person, but it had been clear the photo was an old one.

I didn't let him in right away, though, because there were rules that I needed to hear him agree to. If he didn't, then I would find another guy for the night.

"No questions, no small talk, just sex and then you leave. Deal?"

He smirked before he spoke. "Aye, works for me."

Holy shit, he was Scottish! He didn't

have a thick accent, but he had one and it was the sexiest thing I had ever heard.

I stepped back and allowed him to enter. The second the door was closed, I pushed him back against it and captured his lips. He knew from my profile that I was a top so we didn't need to have the discussion of who was driving or not. Cy easily gave up control and allowed me to dominate the kiss without any fight.

He had a red beard, just a bit more than a five o'clock shadow, and it felt rough against my hand, but that didn't bother me. I was so used to guys being clean-shaven, that the feel of the roughness was a pleasant new sensation against my skin.

As our tongues danced with each other, we both turned our attention to the other's clothes. He was wearing just a t-shirt and jeans so it didn't take me long to get him naked. The second his shirt was off, I ran my hands over his chest and down his chiseled abs. He felt amazing against me and my body was already ready for him.

I pulled him away from the door and brought him over to the bed. He easily lay down and opened his legs for me to fit in between. The second our bodies connected, we both gave a soft moan as our dicks pressed against each other.

I broke the kiss, not wanting to draw this out. We were both here for one thing and one thing only. We didn't need to make out for hours first.

I made my way down his neck, kissing and nibbling his skin as I ground my hips against his. The added friction, the real skin on skin friction this time, caused us both to let out a deep moan. I hadn't gotten to see his dick yet, but he felt big. Something I'd discovered I enjoyed.

I only topped, I held no interest in bottoming. There had been a few guys who'd wanted me to try, but I always turned them down. Even before I'd started to do this, the Grinder hookups, I'd had a few secret boyfriends and I'd never allowed them to top with me. I never wanted a finger inside of me, much less a dick; that just didn't interest me, nor did it make me all tingly at the thought.

What did make me excited was the prospect of a large dick in my mouth. I liked the feeling of it and I liked the control, the power, of knowing I could drive another man wild with need. To make him so desperate for a release that he was willing to do anything for it. I liked being in control. I'd also discovered I liked being a bit rough. Especially recently.

I continued to kiss and lick my way down Cy's chest and made sure to nibble and suck on each of his nipples as I slid further down in search of his hard dick. He was already dripping precome from his slit and my gut instinct told me he was going to be vocal. Some guys found it annoying when their partner was vocal, but not me. I loved it. I could tell how wound up a man was getting by the different sounds they made.

I sucked on his tip, humming my appreciation as the sweet musky taste of him finally hit my tongue. I only gave him a quick suck before I took him all the way down to his base in one go. He was a good size, easily ten inches, but I stopped having gag reflexes long ago.

"Damon," he moaned as he moved his right hand to rest on the top of my head.

I grabbed his hand and placed it back down onto the bed, making sure to grab his other hand to do the same. I didn't like it when someone tried to control me. I was in control and Cy was going to know it. Respect it.

I felt his hands fist in the sheets and I knew he understood that he wasn't allowed to take control. Still, I put my hands on his hips, holding him tightly, my fingers pressing into his skin to make sure he didn't try thrusting into my mouth. He was at my mercy and that was too bad for him if he didn't like it.

He'd have bruises there the next day but that wasn't my problem or something I cared about. He'd known what he was getting into.

I worked all up and down his dick, teasing him and not putting too much pressure on his dick. I wasn't about to allow him to come yet. I wasn't ready for this part to end yet and based on the throaty moans he was giving me, he wasn't ready for it to end either.

I slid my right hand down his hips and around to cup his ass and I was surprised when I felt something brush against my fingers. I pulled my mouth off his dick, Cy letting out a whimper at the loss of contact as I turned my attention to what I felt against my fingers.

"My, my, what do we have here?" I

asked as I pushed the end of the plug, forcing it deeper inside of him.

This wasn't the first time I'd hooked up with a guy who was already stretched or wearing a butt plug. More often than not, when I was in the gay clubs and hooking up in the bathroom or back alley the guy would already be stretched so he wouldn't have to deal with that part of things. It worked for me. It was convenient and made for a quicker fuck. This was the first time a guy had shown up for a booty call with one in, though. Cy moaned as I continued to move the plug in and out of his hole.

"I asked you a question," I demanded.

"My plug," he managed to get out as he started to wiggle his hips and grind himself down against my hand.

I moved my hand back to his hips

and pressed them down as I spoke. "I didn't say you could move." He gave a shiver, but he stopped moving.

I moved my hand back down to his ass and once more started to slowly pull the plug out before pushing it back in as I spoke.

"Good boy. How long has it been in?"

"Six hours."

That shocked me. I was expecting him to say maybe an hour at most.

Now that was exciting.

"Six hours. Well aren't you a naughty whore. You've just been sitting around with this plug inside of your ass all day waiting for when you could get a real dick inside of you?"

"Aye. I like the feeling. Please, fuck me," he begged, and I could tell he was struggling not to wriggle his hips to get better friction. I was purposely missing his sweet spot, just skimming it to wind him up, but nowhere near enough to let him explode.

I moved my mouth down to the crease of his leg and inhaled his manly scent, relishing in the sweaty smell before I moved on to suck on his inner thigh, right by his hip. He let out a long moan as I continued to suck hard at his sensitive skin there and when I pulled back I knew he would have a hickey for the next few days.

A reminder to anyone who fucked him next that I had been there first.

"I'm nowhere near done with you yet."

I would fuck him and I would let him come, but only when I was ready for it. Only when I deemed him worthy of it.

I continued to fuck him with the plug

as I took his cock back in my mouth. He gave another deep, throaty moan and I knew the pleasure was building up within him, but he wasn't going to be getting a release just yet. This was my favorite part, the torment and the teasing, and I was not about to let it slip me by.

As time went on, I could tell that he was growing desperate by the change of his sounds. They were more whimpering and whining now as his need grew to the next level. He was trying to stay still, he was trying to be good, but his body cried out with need and it was getting harder for him to keep his body from instinctively thrusting and wiggling to get more friction. To finally give him what he needed for his release. His dick was rock hard in my mouth and I had no doubt that he was hurting slightly from the hardness. I wasn't going to stop until he broke, though, until he begged, and only then would I give him the release he desperately needed.

"Fuck, please. I need to come, please. Please, let me come, I'm beggin' ye."

There it was.

That's what I needed to hear.

The next time I moved the plug back in, I made sure to hit his prostate dead on, causing him to let out a small scream of pleasure. I sucked on his dick harder, hollowing my cheeks as I continued to hit his sweet spot and after only a moment, he let out a long roar as his cum shot out of him and down my throat. I moaned my appreciation as I swallowed and sucked him for every last drop that his body had for me.

Once he finished pulsing, I carefully pulled the plug out of him and removed my mouth from his dick, giving him one last lick on his tip to catch a few last drops of the tasty treat. I tossed the plug down beside the bed as I reached over to the bedside table and grabbed the condom and lube that I had left there.

Cy was breathing heavily and he had his eyes closed as he tried to calm his body down from the roller coaster ride I had just taken him on. I slipped on the condom and added some lube, coating my latex-covered cock just in case the lube inside of him from the plug wasn't enough.

Cy opened his eyes as I grabbed his legs and hauled them up onto my shoulders, exposing his winking pucker to me. I lined the tip of my dick up with his stretched and needy hole, then I slowly pushed in. I wasn't small and I knew I was thicker than the plug he had been using. He gave a lengthy, sharp cry as I pushed inside of him, his walls welcoming me within their tight grip.

He was so responsive and I loved it.

The second I was buried deep inside of him, I pulled out and slammed right back inside of him. Hard. Fuck, he felt good. He was tight and hot and slick.

Perfect.

I hit his sweet spot dead on and he let out a scream as pleasure shot through him.

"That's it, you naughty whore, let it out," I growled.

"Oh fuck, don't stop," he panted as he reached up and gripped the headboard behind him.

I reached my right hand up and ran the tip of my finger over his swollen lips. He opened his mouth so I took the invitation and shoved my finger inside of it. He moaned as he sucked on my digit, his gaze locked with mine, his hips bucking up against each thrust inside him. I could see the heat in his heavy-lidded gaze and it drove me wild.

He loved this just as much as I did.

He was young, early twenties, so I had to imagine he didn't have much experience with sex. At least not as much as I did. I didn't mind that, though. It meant he'd likely be more into learning and enjoying experimenting, finding out what worked for him, than someone who'd already done it all before.

"Such a good boy," I praised, and he let loose another loud moan at my words.

It would appear Cy had a praise kink.

Nice.

I pulled my hand away from his mouth and he let out a soft whine at the loss of my finger in his mouth. I wrapped my hand around his throat, applying a small amount of pressure, and he whimpered, his gaze glazing over.

He wrapped one hand around my wrist, grasping it tight, but I knew it wasn't so he could pull my hand away or indicating I should stop. I allowed him to keep his hand there as I picked up my pace and pounded hard and deep inside of him. I made sure to hit his sweet spot each time I thrust, and he arched his back in encouragement as skin slapped against skin and my hips punished his ass.

I could feel the walls of his hole getting tighter, gripping my dick, and I knew he was close. I was close too, but I didn't believe in coming before my lover.

"Touch yourself. I want to watch as you come," I ordered.

He sucked in a hissing breath and instantly, his hand went to his hard dick, fisting his length, and he started to jerk himself off furiously. I moved forward so he was more folded into himself, and I knew I was trapping his hand between us, making it hard for him to complete the previous instruction, but it brought me closer to his mouth. I placed my lips close to his, not allowing his lips to touch mine yet but just hovering a hair's breadth over his mouth.

"You like it when I call you a good

boy, don't you?" I asked softly, allowing my lips to lightly skim over his. He went to press his against mine, but I pulled back just enough so he couldn't touch me.

"Aye," he panted.

"I want to feel you come. I want to feel your tight ass milking my dick for every last drop. Now, be my good boy and come for me," I said, as I slammed hard against his sweet spot once more.

That was all Cy needed before he gave a long scream as he came hard and shot his cum all over his stomach. The tightening of his walls around my dick was just the push I needed for my own orgasm to hit. I snapped my hips forward and buried myself deep inside of him as I exploded into the condom. We were both breathing heavily as our dicks pulsed and the wash of our climaxes rolled over us repeatedly.

Once my body calmed down enough, and my breathing had returned to more normal, I moved back and removed my hand from his throat. I slowly pulled out, grasping the edge of the condom, as Cy's legs collapsed down onto the bed. I could see that he was spent, but I didn't believe in cuddling afterward. This was just sex, which meant it was time for him to get going. I climbed off the bed as I spoke.

"I gotta shower. You know where the door is."

I didn't look at him to see what his reaction was, it wasn't important. I headed into the bathroom and closed the door without another word or glance in his direction. It was what we'd both agreed to, so if he had a problem with it, that was on him and not on me. This wasn't going to turn into a relationship from a one-night stand. That wasn't what I was looking for. That wasn't what anyone was looking for off Grinder. We'd had a good time, it was just that simple.

After tossing the condom in the garbage can beside the sink, I turned the shower on and stepped under the hot spray. The night was just getting started and I was looking forward to the rest of it.

CHAPTER TWO

Cyrus

I PULLED OFF to the side of the road as I approached Station Twenty-One. Today was my first shift with them and I should've been excited about it, but all I felt was dirty.

I had brought it on myself. I knew better than to use Grinder for anything meaningful, but last night I wanted to celebrate getting selected to be a Probee at a firehouse. Not everyone who made it through the fire academy actually got chosen by a firehouse. There was not always a position available or the funding for another firefighter and then everyone had to wait in a queue. I was lucky enough to have graduated closer to the top of the list so I was chosen.

I was even luckier to have been picked up by house Twenty-One. I didn't know much about the guys there, but I did know that Captain Clarke was a gay man and he was out and proud. That meant that his firehouse had a zero tolerance for intolerance. It was the type of firehouse a guy like me needed. I was gay, but I wasn't necessarily out. I wasn't in the closet either, though. I lived in this gray area where I was proud to be a gay man, but I wasn't exactly screaming it from a rooftop. If someone asked, then I would tell them the truth, just like if someone asked if I was seeing anyone. But I didn't feel the need to tell everyone that I was gay right from the start.

If no one asked and relationships never came up, then why should I have to tell people?

Straight men and women didn't go around telling everyone they were straight so why should I?

I knew this station was going to be a good one. I knew I wouldn't have to worry about little snide comments or jokes when the guys eventually did discover that I was gay.

My issue was last night and my extreme error in judgment.

I didn't often go on Grinder. I was only on it because every now and then a man got an itch that he needed scratched and sometimes it was just easier to have a quick hook up than to build a relationship. There was a reason why my generation had so many dating and hook up apps.

I had been focused on being in the fire department since I was a kid. When I turned eighteen, I was crushed to discover they weren't taking on any new recruits just yet. They had to live by the budget set out by the city and they were already pushing it, so they couldn't take on any more firefighters. Even with that setback, I didn't let it stop me.

I had gone to work full-time in a shitty, meaningless job and during my free time I spent it working out and running different drills so I would be ready for the academy when it opened up again.

That finally happened this year, just before my twenty-first birthday.

I was down at the recruitment office bright and early on the morning registration opened. I was first in line with all of my paperwork in order, including a full medical exam report that I had gotten the week prior.

When I'd gotten that acceptance letter, I had never felt excitement like that in my entire life. I had worked hard for it and I was finally on the road to living my dream. I pushed myself as hard as I could in the academy so I would stand out. So I could be at the top of my graduating class and so hopefully, I could guarantee a position in a firehouse. And it was all worth every all-nighter and every sore muscle.

So last night I wanted to celebrate.

I wanted to have one last fling before I would need to put all of my time and attention into my new position. I had almost given up hope, but then I came across Damon's profile and I couldn't resist sending him a message. He was sexy and I'd always had a thing for older guys as well. I didn't have much experience in the bedroom, but I did know that the few guys I had slept with who were older than me, they were a hell of a lot better than the guys my age. Older men knew things in the bedroom. They had the experience to truly take a lover on a roller coaster ride of pleasure that left their legs weak for hours afterward and that was exactly what I'd wanted last night.

When Damon rhymed off the rules at his hotel, I didn't think anything of it. I'd heard the same things plenty of times. Hell, I'd said them. But I knew they were never true, at least not fully. Yes, most of the time there wasn't any talking, but afterward there was usually a few minutes of civility, at least. We would normally lie there as our bodies started to come back down to Earth. During those moments there was small talk, there was politeness and the other person eventually saw the other one off at the door with a goodbye kiss. That's what I had expected from Damon.

Only I essentially got a polite *fuck you*.

I felt dirty, used, like I was a prostitute who had given it away for free because a cute guy winked at me. I had never done a walk of shame before, but I did last night and it didn't feel good.

What made it worse, was last night had been the best night of my life.

The sex was incredible. I hadn't even known it was possible to feel that good, to feel that level of pleasure, and now just thinking about it made me feel dirty and cheap. Maybe it was my age or maybe it was inexperience, but I'd never expected to feel that way after sex and I never wanted to feel that way again.

I let out a sigh and shook my head slightly to try and clear my thoughts and emotions. Today was supposed to be a good day, a happy day, and I couldn't let what happened between Damon and I taint this day. I had waited a long time for it and I wasn't going to let anything destroy it.

I reached over and grabbed my bag before I climbed out of my car and walked the short distance to the firehouse. I was really hoping today went well. I knew I would have to pay my dues. I would have to do the smaller tasks that no one would want to do, but I was ready for it. I was ready to cook and clean and grab equipment. I was ready for it all because once the probation period was over, I would be a real firefighter. It would take a year before my probation period was over, but the guys wouldn't be riding me hard the whole time. I just had to prove to them that I was capable and also a team player.

I had this.

Walking inside, I was instantly

looking around. Each firehouse was a bit different in how they had everything setup. Some were older than others as well, but Twenty-One appeared to be one of the station houses that were renovated within the past five years. It looked great and it looked like a lot that I would need to clean. I knew cleaning was going to be one of my daily tasks, but that was fine. It would keep me busy, at least during our downtime.

I made my way toward where the voices were coming from. I walked into a kitchen and living room area. There were five guys, one of which I recognized as Captain Clarke. I didn't really know the others. It didn't take two seconds before they all noticed me. I gave a friendly smile as I spoke.

"Hey, I'm Cyrus MacMillan, your new

Probee."

"And we bagged a Scot," the one man said from his position behind the kitchen counter.

"Great, now Zander will be multilingual with swearing," another guy said and the guys all laughed.

"About fucking time." I was going to assume that was Zander.

Captain Clarke walked over to me as he held his hand out and spoke. "It's a pleasure to have you here. From what I have heard you were top in your graduating class and a real joy to have around. I'm Captain Clarke. This is Zander, Gage, Hawke, and Newt. Newt is our paramedic who has somehow managed to stick around for longer than two weeks."

"Do they normally not?" I asked,

slightly confused.

"The city tends to have paramedics floating from one firehouse to the next. They feel it is the best way to handle having females around the neanderthals who are firefighters." Newt answered, but that did nothing to ease my confusion.

"We are not all Neanderthals," Hawke instantly defended.

"I'm not saying you guys are. The firefighters in this house are all amazing. Everyone tries to get shifts here. Captain Clarke has made this house a safe place for men and women, straight or gay. We all know that we can work here without any harassment. That's not true at most of the other houses, though. I've seen about a dozen female paramedics walk off the job because they couldn't handle the male firefighters' bullshit. It's a serious problem, one that the city doesn't seem all that interested in correcting," Newt fully explained.

"That's terrible. I'm sorry they've had to go through that."

I couldn't believe that paramedics would have to float around because there were too many problems with staying in one firehouse for any length of time. No one should have to go through that and no one should feel like they needed to quit because the job wasn't going to get better. That wasn't fair to any of them.

"So, were you born in Scotland?" Gage asked.

"No, I was born here. My parents were and they came over when my Ma was up th' duff with me. They were visiting some family friends in New York, but a snowstorm grounded their flight. Ma went into labor and a wee bairn was born one month early. By the time they could fly with me, they had decided they didn't want to leave."

"*Up th' duff.* Love it! You are going to be my new best friend," Zander said, flashing me a big smile.

"Hey," Hawke said, clearly insulted.

"What? You know I love you, but he gives me new fun words," Zander said with a playful wink.

"How are your parents with you being a firefighter? You don't look much older than twenty, I have to imagine they are worried," Gage commented.

"My parents are dead. They died when I was sixteen."

It wasn't anywhere near that simple,

though.

My parents had been amazing growing up. I didn't ever remember a time where we went hungry or we didn't have a place to live. They never hurt me, they never hit me, they barely yelled at me or each other. It was a happy home. A home filled with love.

I didn't discover that it was also a home filled with lies until I was sixteen.

I had been in school when my principal pulled me out in the middle of class. I got out into the hallway and saw a detective and the guidance counselor standing there. They took me into the principal's office where they then informed me that my mother was dead and my father had been arrested for her murder. As it turned out my father, Jamie McDougal, was a prolific arsonist who had been responsible for setting over a hundred fires and killing eighty-three people in them.

The last person he killed was my mother.

He had started setting fires not long after they were married in Scotland. Apparently, that was the reason why my father didn't argue with my mother about staying here after I was born. The Scottish police and fire investigators were already getting too close to identifying him over there.

It took the police and fire investigators sixteen years and eighty-three victims before they finally discovered that my father was responsible. They had caught a lucky break via a bird watching camera that caught him starting the fire. The signature was the same as the previous fires and the police had everything they needed to make the arrest. Only somehow my father caught wind of it and he ran with my mother to the Couturie Forest where he doused her with gasoline before setting her on fire. His plan had been to take advantage of the dry weather to start a forest fire that would either kill him or give him the perfect opportunity to escape. Still to this day I was not really sure which outcome my father was rooting for. Either way, he had been captured and convicted. He was sentenced to a hundred and eighteen years. One year for each fire he'd set. Apparently the judge felt like it was poetic justice.

With my mother dead and my father in prison, I didn't have any family over here and I wasn't about to be shipped off to Scotland to live in a country that I had never even been to either. As a minor, I had been placed in a group home where I'd lived for two years before aging out of the system.

Growing up in the group home was horrible for the two years I had to endure being there. I was often bullied or beaten up by the other guys there. Word spread very quickly who my father was and I was bullied and hated at school. Like somehow it was my fault for the sins of my father. Those two years were the hardest years of my life.

The second I turned eighteen, I changed my last name to my mother's maiden name with the hope that I could go under the radar and no one would recognize the similarities in our facial features. So far it had been working, but I was always worried it would come out.

"We're sorry to hear that. It couldn't have been easy for you. Did you live with family afterward?" Captain Clarke asked, and I was relieved that he didn't ask me how they died.

"Group home. My family was all back in Scotland and I had never been. I was an American citizen as well and not a Scot. I spent two years in a group home before aging out."

"I grew up in the foster care system so I know it wasn't easy on you. If you ever want to talk, I'm always willing to listen," Hawke said with an understanding smile.

That was something that I had noticed, a lot of first responders were foster kid survivors. I never referred to anyone that went through the foster care as a victim. We all survived the experience, we all survived our own experiences, and sometimes those experiences could have ended us, but we came out stronger. To me, even the ones who didn't come out stronger, the ones who came out with demons they needed to work through, they were still survivors. That didn't mean it was easy to adapt to the real world. I was lucky, because I had only been in the foster care system for two years. I couldn't imagine having to grow up in it. Before anymore could be said the alarm was going off.

"Engine Fifty-Seven, Ambulance Sixty-One, multiple motor vehicle accident on Freeway Eighteen by Vine Street off ramp."

"All right, let's go, Probee," Zander chirped, flashing me a smile as the guys all started to head out.

I dropped my bag and headed out with them. They all grabbed their gear and I could see my own firefighter's jacket with my name on it hanging up. I grabbed it and tossed on my boots before I ran over to the truck. I climbed into the back with the rest of the guys while Newt headed to the ambulance with his partner.

"That's Jackson driving and this is Sinclair," Zander said with a nod to the other guy who was in the back with us.

"Cyrus MacMillan," I said, flashing them a friendly smile.

"Nice to meet you," Jackson called out from behind the wheel.

"You'll be with Sinclair, he's the

Lieutenant," Captain Clarke informed me.

"I look forward to learning from all of you," I said.

I knew this was going to be a crazy experience and I had no idea how well I would do outside of the academy. The academy prepared recruits to have the skills to be able to handle surviving through their probation year, but they didn't tell them exactly what to expect. It was one thing to be able to handle a controlled fire in a training house and quite another to be involved in a fire that was unpredictable with real lives in the line. To see real people being put in danger and being hurt, killed. There were going to be a lot of rocky days and nights ahead of me, but I was really looking forward to experiencing all of the good that came with it.

The second we pulled up to the accident scene, the guys were jumping out of the truck before it even came to a full stop. I quickly jumped out after them and ran to catch up with the Lieutenant.

"Probee, what do you see?" he asked as the guys started to pull equipment from the truck.

I took a moment to look around and take in the scene as I spoke. "Three cars involved in the accident. Lots of additional cars are still driving. Police are trying to get the lanes shut down, multiple tow trucks waiting for their turn. Skid marks on the ground... so they tried to stop. Three people injured and sitting on hoods of the different cop cars. Two people still trapped in their vehicles, a male and a female."

"What is the most dangerous threat to an accident scene?"

"The gasoline. One spark could make it explode."

"Exactly. In a freeway accident we have to watch out for passing cars. Until the police can get the lanes closed down everyone is in danger. Most cars will go slowly as they pass by, but others will barrel right through and not care if they hit someone. You have to keep your head on a swivel and be aware of your surroundings."

"Aye, Sir."

"When you arrive at an accident scene, you have to have fire extinguishers ready to go in case one of the cars starts to burn. Your priority is to quickly evaluate which victim is the main concern and how to get them out of the car as fast but safely as possible. Every accident victim gets a c-collar, whether you or they think they need it. It's protocol and only a doctor can clear their c-spine. Once a c-collar is on a victim, you never take it off no matter what. If there was damage done to their c-spine, you could have aggravated it and permanently paralyze them. Do I make myself clear?"

"Crystal."

I was more than happy to listen to his instructions and to watch the guys work, but I also wanted to be out there working with them. I wanted to get my hands on the equipment and to help save a life.

"We run things a bit differently. When we can, we like to make sure our Probees get to watch as a real life rescue goes down, then the next time you will be doing it with them. We will also be running multiple drills back at the house. We don't just do fire drills, but accident drills as well. We get old crushed up cars from the tow yard and recreate different scenarios. Today you will be learning how to use the equipment back at the house. We will have you extracting different dummies so you can get a feel for the equipment and best practices. I know it's different to other firehouses, but Captain Clarke and I believe it's important for a Probee to be able to make mistakes without someone's life on the line. Doing complex drills allows you to make those mistakes so when you have to do it in a real life situation, you won't make them and someone won't die."

I could understand that and it seemed like the Captain and Lieutenant had thought their training process through. It was different compared to what I had heard about other firehouses, but I did like the safety net that it provided me. Generally, you had no safety net. You get a call and you do it and just hope that your training is enough. The way they were doing things though, it allowed me to get practice in. It allowed me to learn how the guys do it and the best practices. It allowed me to build muscle memory so when I arrived on scene it would be instinctual and I wouldn't have to think and analyze everything.

"I understand. I look forward to learning everything I can from you and the guys."

And I meant that.

Watching as the other guys worked, I realized quickly that they were a well-oiled machine. They easily worked together, knowing what their partner needed without them having to say anything. It was a fluid dance and in no time they had both of the pinned victims out of their vehicles and on a stretcher. I knew if I was going to be able to stay in their family, I would need to learn how to intermix into their process. It would be a delicate process, but I was hoping that we would all click and I could just become another piece of their machine. I had a lot of work ahead of me, but I was determined to make it happen. I would prove to them that I was the right choice and that I belonged in their family, on their team.

CYRUS

Today was the first day of the rest of
my life and I just knew that it was going
to be one of the best days of my life.

CHAPTER THREE

Damon

I QUICKLY MADE my way through the building to reach my office.

Before Taye had been arrested, I would walk with my head held high and I would speak with my investigators as I walked by. I would check in with them and ask them how their cases were going and offer any support that I could. Now though, I pulled out my phone and kept my head down and made it look like I was too busy to stop and talk. I didn't want to hear any of their sympathy or false claims of hope.

When the news first broke, everyone looked at me like I was the victim and I hated it. I wasn't a victim. Taye didn't hurt me. He'd hurt and killed other people. They were the real victims and I didn't need sympathetic and sad looks being thrown my way. I needed them to focus on their work, on the cases that were left open on their desks. That was what I needed.

Some days, I wanted to scream at everyone to stop looking at me like I was an abused dog. To leave me the hell alone and focus on their work. That I was their Captain and they needed to remember that. I didn't though, because I knew that if I yelled at anyone, I would only be making myself appear unstable. I had to keep up appearances. I couldn't let anyone suspect that I was struggling or not one hundred percent.

The second I was in my office, I let out a sigh. I was safe in here, but I knew eventually someone would be knocking at my door looking for approval on something. I would have to interact with someone soon enough. I knew I needed to get my head back in the game. I knew I needed to get my life back in order and stop being stupid and reckless.

The problem was, I didn't want to yet.

I didn't want to stop drinking and partying. I didn't want to stop having random hookups. I knew what the Shrink would say: I was denied the freedom to be rebellious and to express and explore my own sexuality through normal societal actions of a young adult. Now that my father was dead and the family's reputation destroyed by Taye, I was seizing the opportunity to live out the actions and decisions I never got to have growing up. Which basically translated to me being a drunken manwhore now, because I couldn't do it growing up with all of the other young adults free from their parent's house and control.

I suppose that could be true. I didn't get to be a normal teenager or twenty-something years old. I didn't get to party or go to the bars. Even when I was old enough to drink, I still didn't get to go out and party. My father always told me, told us, that we had to uphold the family name. We couldn't be drunk and sloppy. We couldn't have meaningless hookups that would bring forth unwanted attention and make people question our focus and dedication to the job.

My father refused to accept that I was gay. I had told him, my whole family, when I was fourteen, and he made sure to tell me that I wasn't and never would be. I was never allowed to be around a guy and never allowed to be alone with one. He would even set up dates for me. He would invite a girl over who he felt was suitable for the family name and would be able to handle the life of a firefighter. I would get asked to come over for family dinner and there she would be. Always attractive, always polite, submissive, and completely stupid. I didn't mean stupid in a social sense, no. I meant it in the literal sense. They were always airheads. The type who believed as long as they were attractive everything would be fine. They all only wanted to have a man who would take care of them so they didn't have to work. Their only job was to cook, clean, and be good looking. They were empty of any personality or self-respect.

Even if I was interested in women, I would never have dated them. I wanted someone real. Someone who didn't always need me to be the strong one. I didn't want to have to constantly take care of someone. I wanted someone who I could support and be there for, but someone who could also do the same with me. Someone who could be the strong one when I needed the time to be vulnerable and uncertain. I wanted someone who could have shared interests with me. Someone who was proud of who they were and confident in themselves. I wanted a real person, one that could click with me and we could complete each other. I wanted an equal partner.

I used to think it was possible, but after all of these years, I now know that it was just a fairytale. I was never going to be able to have that with someone, because I was never going to be able to be open and honest about who I was. I was very much in the closet; I was so far in the closet that I could see Narnia. I spent most of my time hanging out with the lion, Aslan.

At first, I had kept my sexual orientation to myself, because I knew as long as my father was alive I was never going to be free to be myself. He was never going to allow or tolerate my coming out publicly. To him, I was a disgrace to the family name and if people knew I was gay, then I would be disrespecting and shitting on our family's legacy and that was something he would never allow.

After his death, I was technically free to be myself, but I had spent so many years too afraid to be honest with people. Coming out seemed terrifying, too terrifying, so I stayed quiet and kept living my life just as I had with him alive.

Like I said, he never laid a hand on us, but he didn't have to in order to keep us in line. He was never short to call me a name for being gay. Every chance he got, he threw it in my face, calling me a faggot or homo. If I didn't get top grades in the academy, it was because I was a fag and needed to screw a woman to be a man. It didn't matter how many times I told him that I was born this way, he refused to believe it. All he cared about was the legacy. *His legacy.* Nothing was more important than honoring that.

It was a good thing he was dead now, so he wouldn't have to deal with Taye. At the same time though, there was a small part of me that wished he was alive so he would have this thrown in his face. He thought it would be me and my sexual deviance that would ruin the family name. I would have loved to see his face when instead it was Taye on the front of every newspaper for multiple counts of arson, homicide, and attempted homicide. To watch as he had to sit in that courthouse and listen to people testifying about the damage Taye had done. To watch as he had no choice but to listen to Tristan's testimony, a gay man's testimony, about his eldest son trying to kill him and a cop. It was petty of me, but I was allowed to think it. It was natural after everything he put me through, that I would want to wipe that smugness off his face.

I strolled over and slid into the chair behind my desk and quickly reviewed at what needed to be done today. I had a bunch of paperwork that needed to be completed and filed before the cases went to court. I also knew that Assistant District Attorney Barba had some documents that he needed me to go over to sign off for him. I had a lot of work that needed to be done and I knew I had to get started, but like every morning, I was finding it hard to get motivated enough to care about any of it.

This morning, I was also nursing a hangover.

After Cy left last night, I had two more guys come over for a party and the three of us enjoyed each other for a good chunk of the night. We drank and the one guy, Jay, brought some cocaine with him. I knew I shouldn't be doing it, but again, I didn't care. It wasn't like I was going to be randomly drug tested, that was only for active firefighters in the field.

Sure, I had a reputation to uphold, not just my family's name, but that of a Fire Captain. I wasn't in the field, but I was still a Captain and was expected not to be doing anything illegal. So if it ever came out that I was using cocaine recreationally, it wasn't going to go well. I was risking my career, my livelihood, but again, I couldn't care enough. It was the weirdest thing, because I knew I had to care. I knew I had to straighten back up and stop drinking so often, stop the drug use and random sex. I knew all of that and if it was one of my guys telling me about the shit that I had done, I would be suspending them and sending them to the Shrink. I was a hypocrite, and I needed to stop, but I couldn't bring myself to do it. I didn't understand why and it wasn't like I could talk to anyone about it.

The few friends I had in the department, they weren't in any position to offer advice and really, I knew what they would say. It would be the same thing I would say to them if they approached me. I knew I could talk to my best friend, Will, but I also didn't want to put him in a compromising position. He was a Captain himself out of the Twenty-First and it wasn't fair to put him in a position where legally he was required to report me to the Upper Brass. I knew he wouldn't, but he couldn't have plausible deniability if he was ever questioned down the line. By not telling him, I was protecting him. At least that was how I was rationalizing it in my mind. Again a Shrink would call bullshit on me, but that was precisely why I was refusing to speak to a Shrink. I had survived this long on my ability to lie to myself and to believe those lies as truths. The last thing I needed, the last thing my psyche could handle, was someone telling me I was a liar and blowing up my whole coping method.

I booted my computer and pulled up my email. I usually had it on my phone, but I'd deleted it once emails started to come in about Taye. After his arrest, the Upper Brass, rightly so, had to release memos and newsletters about the arrest and charges. They had to show their support for Taye, while also being sympathetic to the victims as well as Tristan and Detective West. It was a deadly tightrope that they were walking, because they couldn't outcast Taye without him being officially convicted of these crimes.

If he was found acquitted, never going to happen, but if it did, then technically, he could still come back to work. The Upper Brass couldn't show they were biased one way or the other. By showing support to every party, they were covering their asses while protecting them at the same time. It was a dance that the Upper Brass were very good at, and just another reason why I didn't want to be promoted again. Thankfully, with Taye's arrest there was a very good chance that I would never be looked at for a promotion ever again.

"Fuck off," I said, as I saw the email for a mandatory therapy session with Dr. Keaton Raitt.

I knew it was coming. My boss had told me I should speak with him to be cleared officially for duty. I was never taken off duty, but as ADA Barba pointed out, any defense attorney could call into question my judgment. If I saw the Shrink, then everyone's ass was covered that I was mentally cleared for work and mentally competent, therefore any case I signed off on couldn't be done with ill intentions.

I tried to tell my boss, to convince him that I didn't need to be cleared by a Shrink, that I was fine. My work hasn't diminished. I made sure I got everything done that needed to be done. I never handed anything in late and I had never been late for work or missed a shift. I was always here doing what needed to be done. I didn't need some Shrink poking around in my head, because he would.

It wouldn't be just about Taye being arrested, it was going to be about how I felt about my brother, about my father, about my job, my childhood. He was going to turn it into some bullshit session only to tell me I had deep-rooted childhood issues that needed to be worked on before I could be cleared for work.

Part of me couldn't help but wonder if my boss was trying to push me out. To force me to quit or give the Upper Brass a reason to let me go. That legacy that worked in my favor was now working against me, because now they needed to save face and the best way to do that would be to eliminate the name Amaro. With me being the last one, they didn't have much work ahead of them to get me out. The best way would be to have the Shrink come up with some psychological reason for me to not be fit for duty. From there it was just a short hop, skip, and a jump to my walking papers and the department could save face.

I wasn't going to go that easily, though. I wasn't about to let them push me out. I might not have chosen this career, nor wanted it, but it was mine now and I was not about to start all over again. I was living with this career and doing my best to make it work.

I was too old to start a brand new career and I was not old enough for some midlife crisis. I had no choice but to go. It was mandatory and it would look worse if I didn't show up for it. I was going to have to play this smart, give the Shrink enough insight, but not too much. I could also lie my ass off if he brought up my father or my childhood. Show the Shrink that I was competent and capable of still working. If I did that, then he wouldn't be able to tell my boss that I needed some time off or that I wasn't suitable to work anymore.

I knew the Upper Brass would be coming after me at some point. Taye was a huge black spot on the fire department's record. They needed to cover their asses and clean house. I expected it from them. I just never expected for my own boss to be coming for my job. I thought we were on good terms and that I had his loyalty, but apparently I was wrong. I wasn't about to make that mistake again. I was on my own in this and I wasn't going to forget it.

My phone rang and I looked over to see the name of Taye's lawyer flash across my screen. I hit ignore and sent the call to voicemail. I knew he would leave a message and he knew I wasn't listening to them or I would have called back. He wanted to talk to me, he needed to talk to me, but I wasn't about to do that. I wasn't going to be supporting Taye in court or through the trial. I wasn't even going to go. I wanted no part of that circus and I wasn't going to sit there and listen to Taye trying to reason and excuse his actions or for his defense lawyer to tear apart any of the witnesses.

Not my pig, not my farm, not my problem.

Barba could handle the trial and I would be spending the day getting as drunk as possible. My brother's lawyer would just have to give up and take the hint for the hundredth time. I didn't care what he wanted, but I suspected he was hoping I would testify on my brother's behalf.

But that was never happening.

Even if I believed he was innocent, which I didn't, I still wouldn't be getting up on that stand to testify for him. He was cruel to me growing up and I didn't doubt for a single second that my father had known what he was. He knew and he didn't care about what it could do to everyone else. All he cared about was making sure the family legacy continued. That the family name stayed in good standing.

And now here we were.

All of the good that my grandfather and father did was all in vain now. It was all for nothing because whenever someone Googled the name Amaro they were only going to find the news articles about Taye. All the future firefighters would know was Taye's crimes. They were both rolling in their graves and it served them right, especially my father. He thought his gay son would be the one to bring dishonor to the family, only for it to be the golden boy. It was almost laughable, really.

My grandfather and father were dead, and now Taye was going to prison for the rest of his life. I was finally free of all of them and I was not about to let my newfound freedom go to waste. I just had to get through the trial and the months afterward. Once things calmed back down, then I would be able to focus on myself and not some name on a plaque. Within a year it would all be a horrible nightmare. I just had to last that long.

Thank God for whiskey.

CHAPTER FOUR

Cyrus

TODAY HAD BEEN amazing. It was truly a surreal experience. I was tired, my body was tired, but my mind was wired. I didn't think I could sleep even if my life depended on it. My body was sore from running drills all day and then going on calls.

We didn't have a single fire, but we

had a lot of rescues. The guys said that wasn't uncommon, that some days all they did was go from one fire to the next and some days it was accidents. It was common when it was bad weather for car accidents to pick up, too.

I wasn't upset that there wasn't a fire today. It was a good thing that no one was trapped and dying in our sector, but it would have been nice to get some real life experience using a fire hose. The guys all had a system in place and they were fluid. I knew it would take me some time to work my way into their system, but I couldn't get started if we didn't get to work beside each other in the field.

We did run drills, a lot of drills, but wasn't the same. There wasn't an urgency that was present during a real accident or fire. In a real emergency, everyone has their adrenaline pumping and lives are on the line, real lives and not just dummies. There was a difference and I wouldn't get used to it until I got to experience it enough times. I was hoping tomorrow that I could experience my first fire and get my cherry popped.

I headed into the bar with Newt, Zander, and Gage. They wanted to take me out to the Fire Bar, a bar for first responders. I had never been here before. I didn't even know there was a bar where first responders would all go to. I liked the idea, though. I liked knowing that I could go to a bar and have a drink with guys that I knew, with people who understood the life. I could go and not have to deal with being hit on just because I was a firefighter. It was a place where everyone could just be themselves and if you'd had a bad day, there were people around you who understood how you felt. It was a place where you could celebrate your accomplishments, but also a place where you could mourn the losses and hardships from the day. It was a safe zone and it was something we all needed.

The bar was pretty busy considering it was Monday night. At the same time, it also made sense. It wasn't like we were all working nine to five, Monday through Friday. To some of the guys, today *was* their Friday.

It was a decent size bar; one that could easily fit two hundred people in it. It wasn't fancy and I liked that. Patrons could get beer and shots here. It was a neighborhood friendly bar. It was comfortable, inviting, and it didn't make anyone feel like they couldn't afford to drink here. It was really nice.

I followed the guys over to the bar even as Newt moved off to speak with a group of guys perched around a high-top table. I figured he had worked with them in the past now that I knew that paramedics were floaters.

I still couldn't believe they had to float around and all because it was easier than having to make sure the guys that the female paramedics were around acted appropriately. That blew my mind. It seemed like the Upper Brass just wanted to do what was easier for them and screw everyone else.

I knew I really shouldn't have been too surprised. I had heard enough horror stories about the Upper Brass. Most weren't very open-minded about female firefighters and gay firefighters.

I had been very lucky to get into Captain Clarke's firehouse. I knew no one there would care that I was gay. I still wasn't screaming it from a rooftop, but it was nice to know that I could have a conversation about a guy I was seeing without it turning into a whole social debate.

"What do you think, Probee?" Zander asked.

"It's a nice place. I like it a lot. I can see why it would be your favorite watering hole. Are most people firefighters here?" I asked as I took in the crowd.

"Um..." Zander started as he looked around before he continued. "Mostly tonight, yeah."

His voice was a bit tight, but I didn't press. If there was a story there, it wasn't any of my business. I grabbed my beer and took a sip before I let my gaze wander around the crowd. I doubted I was going to see someone that I knew, but it was possible that I might see some of the guys from the fire academy. When my gaze landed someone that I did know, it was the last person I ever expected to see there.

The guy from the hotel last night was sitting at the other end of the bar. He was by himself and seemed to be drinking a good amount, if the empty glasses in front of him were any indication.

He looked just as sexy as he had last night and I couldn't help thinking about how amazing he had made me feel. The sex with Damon had been the best sex I had ever had, but it also made me feel like a cheap whore with the way he ended things. I knew that was what he wanted. He had told me as much, but it still stung with how I was dismissed.

Even though I was still hurt by it, I couldn't help but ignore the excitement that ran down my spine and ended right at my cock at the sight of him. My body didn't care that my mind and heart might still be hurt by our interaction; all it cared about was how he'd made me feel.

I had to give it to him, too. He could make a guy feel like he was on cloud nine. It was like his body knew mine, like we had done this dance before. He instinctively knew I got off on the praise of being called a *good boy.* I had no idea why I had always had a praise kink but nonetheless it was what floated my boat. I was sure there was some therapist out there who would love to dig into my childhood and obvious daddy issues.

Still, the way he made me feel, I hadn't felt like that with anyone. I wasn't some innocent flower, either. I may only be twenty-one, but I'd been having sex since I was fourteen. I'd always been attracted to older men, too. I don't know why, but I was always more interested in them than someone my own age. I think it was because they were usually more stable and they knew what they wanted in life. There were typically no games with older men.

When I was sixteen, I had tried to date guys my own age, but they were inexperienced and just looking to play head games. That wasn't what I wanted and I went back to dating older guys, guys in their thirties.

The first time I had sex, I was fourteen and it was with my Freshman Science teacher. It was my first year in high school and Science was nowhere near my best subject. It was just after midterms and I had barely passed with a fifty-five percent. I knew I wasn't going to pass the final exam. Mr. Deacon had offered me tutoring sessions after school and on weekends. I had been so happy to have the extra help that I had agreed right away. My parents were thrilled because they weren't any better at science.

We didn't think anything of it, why would we?

Teachers were supposed to help their students when they were struggling. That first tutoring session, he had placed his hand on my thigh and we ended up making out. Afterward, he had told me I was a *good boy* and I remember it made me feel proud and warm on the inside. I wanted to hear it again so during my next tutoring session when he kissed me and wanted to take it further, I didn't tell him no. Within a week we were having sex and a whole new world had opened up to me.

We lasted until the start of the new school year. During that summer though, he took me to all sorts of private parties where I met other older men. So when Mr. Deacon moved on, I just found one of those guys and began having fuck buddies. Sometimes, I would have threesomes with them all weekend long.

That was my life and it got worse after I was in foster care. I've always had a high sex drive. I've always loved the feeling of having a dick inside of me. I can't explain it, I wouldn't want to even if I could, because it was just a piece of who I was and I wasn't about to change it for anyone.

Damon though, he made me feel the way Mr. Deacon had and it'd been years since anyone had ever made me feel that good. It was only natural that my body was suddenly craving his touch.

"Who's that guy at the end of the bar sittin' all alone?" I asked, trying my best to not sound too interested. I didn't know if Damon was out or not and the last thing I wanted to do was out someone.

Zander looked over real quick before turning his attention back to me. "That's Captain Damon Amaro. He's the Captain for the Investigation Unit."

Captain?

Fuck.

How was this even possible?

The best sex I'd had since I was bloody fourteen and the man was a Captain within the Fire Department. It didn't matter that he ran the Investigation Unit, a Captain was a Captain, they all had the power to end your career and I had gone and slept with one.

The other oddity that hit me was that Captains worked Monday to Friday, so why the hell was he getting plastered on a Monday night?

He wasn't around anyone; he had

purposely kept to himself in the corner at the bar. He didn't want company, clearly, but he didn't seem to want to sit at home and drink alone either. As if being at home drinking oneself into oblivion on a Monday night was somehow better than doing it at a bar.

"He doesn't seem like he is in a good mood," I commented, trying to calm my racing heart.

Damon had yet to look my way and I was hoping I might be able to avoid eye contact with him for the rest of the night. My dick didn't like that idea though, as it was already starting to swell behind my zipper. The monster was hungry, but that was too bad for it, because I was not about to go over to a Captain who had fucked my brains out and chat him up with the guys from the firehouse here. I had no idea if the Captain would even acknowledge my existence, but I wasn't about to find out.

"He's been going through some stuff. It's best to keep a wide berth from him. Cap is best friends with him so we see him at the firehouse at times, but not too often, especially recently. You ignore him, he'll pretty much ignore you as long as you don't give him a reason to look your way."

That did nothing to ease my concerns about the drinking. Not that I was anyone to be lecturing on drinking or reckless decisions. I was twenty-one and could finally legally drink, but I had started when I was young too, just like every other teenager.

Especially a teenager in foster care.

Just like drugs. Some of the parties I

had gone to with whatever guy I was with at the time, it wasn't uncommon to see bowls of ecstasy and cocaine on different tables. I could understand better than anyone the desire to forget. I wasn't judging Damon and I wished I could say that it made him less attractive, but the exact opposite happened.

I had a thing for damaged men. Also closeted married men that were completely emotionally unavailable. I was a sucker for punishment and I never learned my lesson.

"Duly noted," I said with a nod.

Zander picked up his beer and gave a nod toward the opposite side of the room, even further away from Damon's eye line.

I was torn between hoping he

wouldn't see me and hoping that he would. I knew the likelihood of him acknowledging me was slim to none. He was most likely going to dismiss me like some common street whore, but I wanted his eyes to catch mine. I wanted to see if he would recognize me or if he had already forgotten about our time together.

Just the thought of him not remembering me, it cut deep. It shouldn't bother me, I knew that. I was sure there were plenty of one-night stands that I'd had with guys who wouldn't remember me. There had been ample hook-up nights where me and whatever partner I'd picked up for the night had both been very drunk and I could barely remember anything the next day. It shouldn't bother me if

Damon didn't remember me, but it did.

For the next couple of hours, my gaze kept trailing back over to Damon. He was still at the bar, still drinking. I thought at one point he had left, but he only went to the bathroom before returning to his stool and resuming his drinking, staring off into space.

It was just after midnight when Zander finally called it a night. I hadn't meant to stay that long. I'd only wanted to come out for a couple of beers before heading home. The guys wanted to show me the bar and it was vital for me to get to know them outside of work. Still, I should've already been home and in my bed. I had just worked a twelve-hour shift and I had another one in the morning.

With Zander gone and Damon still

here, I decided to stop being a chicken and mentally torturing myself. He was either going to remember me or not. He was either going to be pleased to see me or not. Either way, I wasn't going to get an answer until I manned up and went over to see him.

Letting out a deep breath, I made my way across the bar, which was drastically less crowded now, and over to Damon. Once I was there, I leaned my back against the bar and kept my eyes on the wall across from me. I was too afraid to look him in the eye right now, not until I knew what he was feeling.

"Of all the bars, in all of the towns," I started.

"I was wondering if you would get the balls to come over and say hello. You've been looking my way since you walked in," he said in a slightly harsh tone, but I didn't take it personally. He did have a lot to drink so far.

"I wasn't certain you would want me to come say hello."

"What house?" he asked.

"Twenty-One with Captain Clarke, but I guess you already know that part. Zander, one of the guys, told me who you were. I swear, I didn't know before last night." The last thing I wanted was for him to think I had targeted him in some way.

"You're the new Probee. No one can know."

Not surprising.

"I would never tell anyone. What happens in my personal life is no one's business. I'm not in the closet, but I don't scream it from every rooftop either.

I don't think it's anyone's business if I'm gay. No one straight has to tell people they are straight, why should I?"

He took a drink from his whiskey before he spoke. "You're gonna walk out the front door, turn right, walk three blocks, take another right, and go into the abandoned factory. I'll be there in five minutes," he said with a slight demand to his voice.

"Is that an order, Captain?" I asked, as a tingle ran down my spine.

"Not professionally. If you decide not to, no hard feelings. Choice is yours."

His husky, whiskey-soaked voice did things to my insides that I couldn't even describe. It might have technically been my choice, but there really was no choice to make. My body was already screaming yes.

I made my way out of the bar, the heavy wooden door closing behind me and cutting off the sound of the music and laughter. I paused for a moment in the sudden quiet and then turned right. I knew it was crazy, going to meet up with a Captain in an abandoned factory to have sex, but it honestly wasn't the craziest thing I'd done. I knew it could be dangerous and come back to bite me in the ass, but I was also a strong believer that the best fun in life tended to be the riskiest.

A part of me also knew how stupid the idea was going to be on a mental level. I doubted Damon was going to get all warm and fuzzy on me, which meant I would be feeling like a cheap whore again. A very satisfied whore, but a whore nonetheless. I should care, but all

I could think about was the pleasure that Damon was going to be giving me.

When I arrived at the abandoned factory, I didn't have to wait long before Damon arrived. He was clearly drunk, but he was still able to function. The man could certainly hold his liquor and I couldn't help but wonder if he had some Scottish in him.

"Strip," he ordered.

I kicked my boots off and started to remove my clothes, but he didn't strip. Apparently, I was going to be fully naked for this. I was hoping he would get naked as well, but I couldn't be certain that he would. He stood there and watched as I stripped, never taking his eyes off of me, and I suddenly felt like I was his prey. It should have bothered me, but it only made my dick pulse with need.

"On your knees," he ordered in that husky, spine-tingling voice once I was naked.

I got down on my knees as he pulled his shirt off. Leaning against a post roughly twenty feet from me, he unzipped the front of his jeans and pulled out his hard dick. His oh-so-glorious dick. He was the biggest man I had ever been with before and I instantly recalled how he felt wonderful inside of me.

My mouth watered at the thought of getting to feel that huge cock sliding along my tongue, pushing against the back of my throat. That was something I missed out on last time and I was really hoping I would get to this time around.

"Crawl over here and suck my dick,

whore," he ordered in a dark tone.

He seemed to really like that word, *whore*. It should have pissed me off. Hell, I'd punched guys in the mouth for calling me a whore or a slut before. Yet, when he said it electricity overtook my body and all I wanted to do was please him.

Without allowing myself to think too deeply on it, I let a groan slip from my lips as I started to crawl toward him. I could see the arousal heating up in his gaze as I got closer.

He loved this part.

He loved the control and dominance.

It made sense with him being a Captain. He would be telling people all day long what to do.

The second I was close enough to him, I took his cock in my grip and brought his tip to my mouth, moaning as the sweet taste of him hit my tongue. He threaded his fingers through my hair, grabbing a fistful in a tight grip. He started to push my head down his shaft as he spoke.

"You're gonna be my good whore and take it all."

I couldn't help but moan, a shiver running though me and straight to my balls at his words. It should terrify me that he wanted me to take him down to his base. This man was not small and I had never deep throated before, which I would essentially have to do in order to get his size in my mouth.

He pushed my head down inch by inch and didn't allow me to pull back to try and catch my breath. I should have been scared, but I wasn't. My dick kept pulsing knowing that this man had complete control over me. He was giving my body everything it had been craving.

"Good boy. Relax your throat. That's it, you can take all of Daddy's dick. It's going to slide right down that pretty, tight throat of yours."

The moan that escaped me was not human. Never, not once, had anyone ever referred to themselves as Daddy with me before. It shouldn't have elicited that much of a reaction out of me, but it did. Fuck, I'm sure a Shrink would love to dissect that one. Just chalk it up to more unresolved daddy issues.

Fuck it; those issues would still be there tomorrow.

I did as I was told and relaxed my throat and if I didn't think about it, it was easier to take him deeper. The second he bottomed out, he let out a deep moan and I could tell he was very pleased with me.

"Such a good whore you are. You have no idea how beautiful you look with my dick down your throat," he growled, fisting my hair even tighter.

He started to lightly thrust his hips and I knew he was going to fuck my throat. I couldn't stop moaning at the sensation of his dick sliding up and down my throat. It shouldn't have felt this good, but the faster his hips went, the more I was moaning and silently begging for more.

I gave a start, whining as I felt myself come in my pants. He had made me come without even touching me. I had never come like that before. I didn't even think it was possible to come from a blowjob and yet this man had done the impossible.

"Naughty whore, Daddy didn't give you permission to come. Now I have to punish you," he said with a slight edge to his voice and it only caused me to whimper again as need rushed through me.

Fuck, this man should not be this sexy. The control he had over me should not be this strong. It was like he knew exactly what my body needed, what it craved, even though I didn't even know it.

"You want Daddy to punish you. All dirty whores do. Don't worry, I'm going to punish you just as soon as I come down your throat."

His thrusts started to become faster, harder. I could tell he was close, that his body was on edge just as much as mine was. Even though I had just come, I was already rock hard again and in desperate need for more.

After a few more thrusts, Damon snapped his hips forward and buried his dick fully down my throat. I had felt a guy come before plenty of times in my mouth, but I had never felt a guy's dick pulsing in my throat. The sensation should have been weird, but it only made me moan and writhe even more.

I already knew I was addicted to this, addicted to this man. It was like he was made for me or I was made for him. God, this couldn't be the last time we did this. I needed more from him and I seriously doubted I would ever get tired of this man.

I greedily swallowed every single drop

he had for me before he was pulling out. I whimpered at the loss, but he didn't care. His hand left my hair and wrapped around my throat and he pulled me up and in for a rough kiss.

I easily gave up control to him and melted against his tongue. I was vaguely aware that he was moving backward toward some large wooden crates that had been left in the factory. When my back hit the rough wood, he pulled back from the kiss and roughly turned me around.

He used one end of his belt and cinched it around my neck before he pulled my arms back behind me and wrapped the rest of the thick leather around both of my wrists, making it impossible for me to move my hands. He then roughly pushed me down, bending me over the crates and kicking my legs out, spreading them as far apart as possible before he spoke.

"Naughty whores get punished. You're not allowed to come, do I make myself clear, whore?" he growled in my ear.

"Aye."

The sharp slap to my ass was unexpected and I couldn't help the small scream of surprise. "It's yes, *Daddy.*"

"I'm sorry. Aye, Daddy," I moaned, my accent more pronounced now that I wasn't as focused on keeping the lilt from my voice.

Fuck, this shouldn't be this hot, what the hell was wrong with me?

I heard the foil of a condom being torn open and I felt my excitement and arousal increase. I needed him badly and I was desperate to feel him inside of me again. I expected to feel his finger against my hole, but to my surprise and pleasure, it was his tip. Apparently stretching was overrated tonight. That was fine with me, I liked the slight burn and I had slept all night with a plug in, so it wasn't like I hadn't had sex in a few months.

He was slow at first as he entered me and I couldn't help the needy moans that poured out of my mouth as I felt his girth stretch the tight ring of muscle. He pushed in until I felt his balls against my ass, seating himself inside me fully. I was breathing heavily as my body adjusted to his size.

He placed his left hand on my hip and then wrapped his right hand around the middle part of the belt that was slung along my back before it reached my wrists. I didn't even have a chance to adjust to his size before he was pulling back on the belt, forcing my throat to constrict, cutting off the air. I arched my back quickly as he pulled almost all the way out and slammed right back in.

His pace was hard, deep, and fast. He wasn't holding back at all as he chased his pleasure, his cock just skimming past my sweet spot each time. Enough to make me hard and throbbing, but not enough to get me off. He was doing it on purpose, he knew exactly where my sweet spot was and he was avoiding it to punish me for coming without his permission. That should infuriate me, but instead it had me in even more of a desperate state.

"Fuck, Daddy," I moaned as I neared

yet another climax.

As if he sensed my approaching release, the hand that was on my hip slid around and suddenly squeezed the base of my dick as hard as he could, effectively killing the orgasm that had been building.

"Naughty whores who don't listen to their Daddy don't get to come."

"I'm sorry, Daddy," I whined, feeling the loss intensely for only a moment before the feeling again began to build in my balls.

He moved his hand back to my hip and continued his brutal pace, grasping my hips tightly and pulling me roughly backward toward him with each thrust. I knew I would likely have bruises there tomorrow but I didn't care.

My legs were trembling from the need

coursing through me and I was desperate to come. Every time I got close, and my balls pulled up tight against my body, that special tingle beginning to rush through my spine, he would wrap his hand around my dick and squeeze like his life depended on it.

I was going insane with need, almost delirious now as the intensity of the edging and orgasm denial rushed through me continuously. My moans and whines were echoing off the factory walls and I was certain someone three blocks away could hear me.

"Please, Daddy, I need to come, please let me come," I begged when he stopped me for the fourth time.

"Shut up and take your punishment like a good boy," he growled and I knew I wasn't going to get to come until he was ready to come as well. Hell, maybe even after.

His thrusts started to become more erratic and frantic. I knew he was getting close and I foolishly hoped that meant I would get to as well. With a loud groan, he snapped his hips forward and I could feel his dick pulsing inside of me, the heat from inside the condom filling me and sending chills rushing through me.

I suddenly had this uncontrollable urge to feel him coming without the condom. It was surprising, because I'd never had sex without one. I was always careful about that. And yet, there was this urge to be owned by him. As if him coming inside of me would somehow make me belong to him. It was ridiculous and yet that need only grew with each pulse I felt.

When he finished, he pulled out and I thought for sure that it would be my turn. I heard him pulling his pants back up and then he was removing his belt from me. I was hoping that I wouldn't have any bruises around my neck and wrists tomorrow. That wasn't something I would be able to explain away very easily. With myself free, I stood up and turned to face him. He had walked away and was putting his shirt back on.

"Get dressed," he ordered.

"What?" Surely he was joking. I was standing here rock hard, dripping with need. There was no way I was getting dressed without coming first.

Damon walked back over to me and placed his hand around my throat. The grip wasn't tight, but it was possessive.

"Did you think me fucking you was

your punishment? You came without my permission and now you will get dressed and you will go home. What you won't do is touch yourself. You don't get to come again, not until I allow it. Either you play by my rules or we don't play, *whore*."

A shiver ran right down my spine and I knew I had never wanted someone so badly before in my life. This man should be all wrong for me. I should be telling him off like a good Scot does, but instead, I wanted to drop to my knees and await my next order.

Fuck, how could one man have such a strong influence on me?

How could he have this type of power over me and all we'd done was have sex twice?

I'd been with guys for a year or more and if they ordered me to do something I would laugh at them.

What made Damon so different?

"Aye, Daddy," I said in a whisper of a voice.

He pulled back and pulled out his cell phone and spoke before handing it to me. "Put your number in."

I easily took the phone and entered my number in the contact screen that he pulled up. Normally, I would call or text myself, but apparently he didn't want me to have his number. It was another way he could control the situation. Control was obviously very important to Damon and I couldn't help but wonder if he was always like this or if something had made him change.

After I entered my number, I handed the phone back to him. He ran his index finger along my hard shaft and I hissed at the pleasure.

"You're going to get dressed and go home. And if you want to be Daddy's good whore, you won't touch yourself, you won't come. And maybe next time, if you are my good boy, I'll reward you by sucking your dick and swallowing every last drop that you have for me."

I let out a deep moan as his finger ran over my tip, gathering the pearl of wetness there, and he brought his digit up to suck on for a moment to get the precum off of it. Before I could even form words, he was leaving.

I stood there watching as he walked out of the factory, unable to move to even get dressed. This night had been very intense and I didn't want for it to end. I wanted to come, but I knew I wasn't supposed to. I also couldn't stand here all night long. With no other choice, I got dressed and strolled out. Tonight was one for the record books and I was truly hoping there would be another round.

CHAPTER FIVE

Damon

THIS WAS BULLSHIT. I shouldn't be sitting here. I shouldn't have to go through this. It wasn't me who started the fires, that was Taye. I shouldn't have to be forced to see a Shrink. I didn't need it. I didn't need to talk about what Taye had done. I didn't need to talk about my father or the legacy that was associated with my name. And I sure as shit didn't need to talk about the drinking or recreational drug use. More than anything, I didn't need to talk about the astonishing sex that I had last night with Cy.

I still can't believe he's a firefighter, a rookie firefighter. He is twenty-one, which I suspected, but I didn't expect for his Captain to be my best friend. The only true friend that I had within the department. Multiple red flags had been raised and I knew I had to walk it back.

We could never hook up again. Not that I had been planning on it and yet, by the end of the night my dick was down his throat and buried in his ass. I knew I was pushing his limits. I had always enjoyed taking control in the bedroom. I had always enjoyed being the boss and I had always found guys who were good with it.

The way Cy responded to my touch and demands though, thrilled me to no end. He was begging for it and more. He loved being dominated and submissive. He loved having a dick in him, whether that was his mouth or his ass. The man was the perfect sex partner and my body was already craving him. I could go for days straight and never get bored of being inside of him.

Addiction much?

I had no idea if he had listened to my order. He could have easily gone home and jerked off. It wasn't like I would know if he did. I was hoping he didn't, though. I was hoping that he had spent the night laying there with a raging hard on for hours until he fell into a restless sleep. I wanted him to be going crazy for my touch. To be in so much need that if I decided to text him for another round, he would drop everything and come over.

I hadn't thought I would want to have an ongoing relationship with anyone, but with Cy it was certainly appealing to me. I just knew we were only scraping the surface of what we could be like with each other. The lengths we could go, the lengths that *I* could go. He was a wet dream and I wanted to explore more with him.

I didn't tend to use Daddy in the bedroom, at least not as a rule. I had in the past, but usually it was Captain, Sir, or Master on the rare occasion. For some reason though, Daddy just flowed right off my lips with Cy and I could tell he didn't have a problem with it. The way he moaned *Daddy* every time he said it, I could tell he loved it and I somehow knew I wasn't the first older man he had been with.

Some guys preferred older men because they were more experienced in the bedroom. I was going to assume Cy did as well. But I could definitely tell he had a daddy kink, along with his praise kink. They did go hand in hand in most instances, and I was sure a Shrink would tell me it was because the guy had some daddy issues to work through.

I didn't care what his issues were as long as he wanted to play by my rules, and Cy seemed very open to my rules.

I had done some pretty reckless things in my lifetime, but sleeping with Cy again might actually top the list. I was not out of the closet and I had no interest in coming out of it. Not even Will knew I was gay. I was putting myself in the position to not only be outed, but to potentially lose my job.

We weren't in the same department, so it wouldn't be wrong for us to date, wouldn't be a direct conflict that way, but the age difference was an issue, not to mention the ranking. I was a Captain and he was a Probee, it would be like an attending doctor sleeping with an intern. It was unethical and career suicide.

Even though I knew all of that, my body was still craving him. I had to jerk off this morning just to be able to get my pants done up. My sex drive felt like it was in overdrive and all I wanted to do was be buried inside of him. I had told myself it wouldn't happen again, but I knew that was a lie. I was going to be having sex with Cy again, many times. I just had to make him wait a bit longer. I wanted his need, his desire for me to explode out of him when I finally did touch him.

I took a drink from my coffee. I was feeling the hangover this morning and I was really hoping that Dr. Raitt wouldn't notice, or he'd at least have the common courtesy to not call me out on it. I doubted he would offer me that courtesy, but I could hope.

There was nothing worse than a psychiatrist appointment first thing in the morning. It was a great way to ruin your entire day. I'd never actually had to speak with Dr. Raitt in a professional capacity before. I'd had to refer to officers under my command to him many times, though.

I almost sent Tristan his way before he solved the arson cases that implemented Taye. I did send him to Dr. Raitt after he had almost died and before he could be cleared for active duty again.

Dr. Raitt had cleared Tristan and he was going to be back to work within the next week or so. He was cleared medically and I was relieved to hear that his lungs were back to one hundred percent. I was thankful that Tristan was going to be okay.

I had never been in a fire myself, but I did know that smoke inhalation was extremely dangerous, especially if you have a history of being in a fire unprotected like Tristan had been. It was going to be good to have Tristan back. He really was my best investigator and I needed him back to work.

The door opened to Dr. Raitt's private office and he stood there in the doorway with a warm and friendly smile plastered on his face. I had a strong urge to punch him right across his stupid face. I couldn't help but wonder how many times he'd actually been hit.

Dr. Raitt wasn't a very large man. He was around five foot eight, but only a hundred and forty pounds, at most. I knew that he was a runner, so that accounted for his lithe, compact form. He was active, but he didn't have any bulk to him. He often volunteered to do the charity runs and marathons for the department fundraising, which was admirable. He was always clean-shaven and kept his hair mostly short, but it had a bit of length to it. Enough that you could run your fingers through his hair and mess it up. He was attractive and I knew he was gay. I'd seen him with his fiancé out at the bars or charity events. From what I'd heard, he was an all around decent guy and most people weren't bothered by his position as the firehouse therapist. Apparently he was super easy to talk to.

Under normal circumstances, I would be happy to have a chat with him, just not about my issues or myself. I was a firm believer that therapy was good for some people, but I didn't believe I was one of those people. I didn't need to talk something to death. I didn't need old issues brought up and examined, dissected. What I needed was a stiff drink and to push through. Erase and override. It worked for me and I was not about to let a pretty face change that.

"Captain Amaro, please come in."

I pushed up out of my seat and made my way over to him. He closed the door behind me and spoke as he made his way over to one of the chairs that were set up in the room.

"Late night?" he asked, with a nod to my to-go cup.

"You don't drink coffee in the morning, Doc?" I countered, not even bothering with sitting down.

"I do. But when you have that large of a to-go cup and you look like you've barely slept three hours, that tends to make me think it was a late night. Do you often drink on a Monday night?"

Fuck this.

I was not going to be doing this dance with him. I knew why I was here. The Upper Brass wanted a reason to push me out. To force me to leave so they could pretend like the Amaro name didn't exist. I was not going to play this game with any of them. If they wanted me out, they could grow some balls and come say it to my face. I didn't have the time or patience for this shit.

"I'm not doing this with you," I said with an icy edge to my voice.

"Doing what, Captain?" he asked patiently, his voice completely calm and controlled, and that only pissed me off more.

"You think I don't know what this is really about? I know the Upper Brass wants me out and they are doing it through you. This is all just a show, a formality so they can fire me with an iron clad defense. Once the Shrink says you are unstable, out the door you go. If they want to take my shield, then they can come down to my office and do it themselves instead of sending a puppet to do it."

Dr. Raitt held his hands up in a mock surrender before he spoke. "Okay, I have no idea what is going on right now. I don't know what the Upper Brass wants or about anyone coming after your shield. What I do know, is that I was asked to speak to you to make sure you were doing okay with the bombshell that was dropped on you. I'm not reporting back to anyone if I think you are suitable to continue working. We're just here to talk. I hear your worry and concern though, and if it eases those worries then I will let you know that with you being a desk jockey, it is extremely difficult for the Upper Brass to push you out. Any psychological issues that you have or are trying to work through, as long as I don't believe you are a harm to yourself or others, there is no reason why you can't keep working."

It sounded good and I wanted to believe him, but it wasn't that simple. I didn't know him well enough to trust him. I didn't know him well enough to know where his loyalties lay. I had looked through the department's policies and bi-laws and I wasn't able to find anything that would give the Upper Brass grounds for terminating my employment with the fire department. However, I also knew that loopholes could be found and political connections could be used. He was saying all of the right words, but that didn't mean I could believe them. I knew that made me sound paranoid and it wasn't a good look to have when you were trying to convince a Shrink that you didn't need therapy.

"You really expect for me to believe we're on the same side?"

"We don't know each other on a personal level, Captain, but you have worked with me before with your other investigators. When was the last time you received a recommendation from me that dictated you remove one of your investigators from the field or their position? I don't believe in taking someone's career and purpose away. I believe in helping my patients to heal and become stronger. To not allow their trauma to have full control over them. I'm not your enemy. I'm here to make sure you can keep doing your job without being destroyed by it. Please, Captain, will you just sit down and we can talk about anything."

Every fiber in my being was telling me this was a trap. That he was trying to get me into a false sense of safety before he would pounce. Like a lioness that leaves one gazelle alone only to come up behind it and rip its throat out. Standing there, refusing to sit and listen, it wasn't helping my case. I had to keep my composure. I had to keep myself in control and calm, otherwise he would think I was too unstable to work.

Resigned to at least try it his way, I sighed and strode over to sit on the couch, keeping my eyes on him. I did my best to school my features so he couldn't read into my emotions.

"What do you want to talk about?" I

asked, trying to keep my voice even.

"It's not about what I want to talk about, Captain, it's about what you want to talk about. We can talk about your family, any cases that you are having problems solving with your guys. We can talk about the weather, your favorite coffee or drink. I don't care what we talk about, as long as we talk."

He was trying to build trust, to build a rapport. He wanted me to let my guard down and that was when he would strike, but I wasn't going to let it happen. I would placate him, but I wasn't going to fall for his tricks.

Once again, I knew that line of thinking made me sound crazy, but I knew people were gunning to have me removed from my job. I had made enemies before this. Having the title of a legacy worked in my favor but it also worked against me. There were people who resented my grandfather and father and would have loved nothing more than to destroy the reputation they had built. Myself and Taye had always been told by our father to not trust anyone and to always watch our backs. It had been drilled into us that you never knew when the knife was coming for you, so stay aware. I couldn't exactly be blamed for waiting for that knife to finally come my way.

"My coffee order is pretty boring," I said, lifting my shoulder in a small shrug.

"Mine as well. My favorite drink though, is scotch. A nice glass of scotch at night after a long hard day at work can always help me relax. What about you? I bet you are a whiskey man."

I used to be just a whiskey man, but now I was more of a liquor man. If it had alcohol in it, I was drinking it. It didn't matter if it was vodka, whiskey, gin, tequila, or even that flavored shit that most women drink. If it had the power to get me drunk, I was all for it.

"I like whiskey," I simply said.

"How often do you drink?" he asked gently, as if it was some horrible thing to do.

"Never on shift, so why does it matter?" I countered.

"I'm not saying it does matter. I was just asking. You look a bit hungover today. I was just curious how often you drink during the week. Look, I'm not asking for you to reveal your deep dark secrets to me here. I just want to talk so

I know how you are handling the bombshell that got dropped in your lap. This is our first session and realistically, we are going to be seeing each other two times a week for the next couple of months."

"Hold up, what?" I snapped.

Months?

Like fuck.

I wasn't going to be doing this for months. I thought I would just have to come here once and then I'd be done. I wasn't going to be talking to a Shrink for months. I wasn't unstable. I didn't need therapy. It wasn't me who set fire to those houses. It wasn't me who killed all of those people. I didn't deserve to be punished like this.

This was so much bullshit.

"Whether you wish to admit it or not,

either out loud or to yourself, you have experienced a trauma. The arrest of your brother, what he was arrested for, that is a trauma and you need to work through it. I can tell you haven't been sleeping properly. I can tell that you have been drinking more often. We might not have known each other very well before all of this, Damon, but I do know you were not a man who drank during the week. You've always had control over yourself and how you presented yourself. You have been hiding it well, but I'm trained to see when someone is struggling. It's okay for you to not be okay right now. That doesn't mean you can't still work. I'm not recommending that you take a leave of absence. All I'm asking is that you are open and honest with me so we can work through the trauma and get you back to being fully healthy. As long as you can do that, I will go to the mat for you should the Upper Brass ever try and take your shield."

Slowly, I let out a deep breath. I had to try and think about this rationally, even though everything inside of me was screaming to run out of here and give Dr. Raitt the middle finger. I knew I couldn't do that, though.

Currently, he was looking to do these sessions while allowing me to work. If I fought him on it, that was likely to change and I would be trapped in my condo staring at the walls. That was the last thing I wanted. The last thing I could handle right now. I had no choice but to play ball right now. To bide my time and do the minimum needed so I could keep working.

"I don't drink every night. It doesn't affect my work, so what does it matter if I drink at night?" I challenged.

"I'm not saying it does matter. I think after what you have been through it's only natural that you are struggling. It's natural that you would be drinking more frequently right now while your mind tries to process the trauma you are going through."

"You keep saying that, *trauma*. I'm not going through trauma. The people my brother burned alive, they have trauma. Their loved ones have trauma. Nothing bad happened to me."

I wasn't a victim in this and I was not about to let anyone call me a victim. I wasn't hurt by Taye's actions. I got caught in the crosshairs, but I didn't experience any trauma.

"People don't like that word, especially men. It's even worse when you add in an alpha male in a male dominated career, such as a Captain in the Fire Department. The truth is though, Captain, you did experience a trauma by what your brother has done. You weren't in the fires. You weren't hurt physically, but you were still hurt emotionally and most definitely mentally. Just because Taye is your brother, doesn't change that it has affected you negatively and that is called trauma. If it didn't affect you, if it hadn't traumatized you, then you wouldn't be spending your nights getting drunk. And I think it's safe to assume that you are also participating in other risky behavior and being promiscuous. There's nothing wrong with that. It's perfectly natural for you to be acting out. For you to be letting off some steam and taking a break from being yourself. I want you to know though, eventually, you will have to find your way back to your true self, and I'll be here to help you," he said, flashing me a small warm smile.

There was no judgment in his voice. He didn't look disappointed or disgusted with me. I didn't tell him anything and yet he was able to figure out that I was different. That I had been acting differently and feeling lost. I wasn't certain how I felt about him knowing me so well after only spending ten minutes with me. We had never spoken like this before. Nothing more than just a polite hello in the hallway as we passed each other. I couldn't help but wonder if he had been watching me these past three months.

If he had, then were others watching me?

Could other people tell that I wasn't fully myself?

That thought was unnerving, because I was supposed to be stable, strong. The people who worked underneath me needed to be able to trust me and rely on me. They couldn't rely on someone if they thought they were unstable.

I had to always be the strong one. I needed to pay more attention to my appearance. I needed to pay more attention to how I was presenting myself and interacting with others. I couldn't let people think I was going weak, that wouldn't be good for anyone's cases.

"I'm fine," I instantly denied.

He gave me that warm smile once

again before he spoke, "No, you're not. But you will be."

He sounded so confident that I would be able to be fine one day. That I would be able to stuff myself back into that box that I had broken out of three months ago. It seemed impossible, and truth be told, I still didn't know if I wanted to be in that box ever again. For now though, I would let him think that was my goal. For now, I would let him think that he was helping and I was doing what I was supposed to be doing. What he didn't know, it wouldn't hurt him.

And if it hurt me, well, that was my business, too.

CHAPTER SIX

Cyrus

"YOU LOOK GOOD," Zander said, flashing me a smirk as he walked into the main area of the firehouse.

I was currently trying to stay awake while sitting on the couch. I shouldn't have stayed out that late, but it was well worth it. I had spent the rest of the night trying to get some sleep. My dick had stayed hard even after I got home and what little sleep I did get was filled with naughty, delicious dreams of Damon.

I didn't jerk off. I could have and I knew I could have. There was no way for Damon to know if I had jerked off or not. As long as I didn't tell him, then he wouldn't have known. Not to mention I didn't know if we would ever get to hook up again. The ball was in his court and that was exactly what he wanted. I was fine with it, though. There was a serious excitement within me at the prospect of getting a text from him to go and meet him.

I wanted to meet him again. I wanted to have sex with him again. More than anything, I wanted for him to tell me I could come. My balls were heavy and swollen from the serious case of blue balls I had. I had no idea if Damon and I were now fuck buddies or if it was just a two-night stand, but I was really hoping we would get to hook up again. The man might not be all warm and fuzzy, but he sure knew how to make a man purr.

It also helped that I could tell he was going through something. Everyone at the bar seemed to avoid him and it wasn't because he was a Captain. Something else was going on that everyone seemed to know about, everyone *but* me. I knew I shouldn't be asking, that it was none of my business and I had no place in asking, but at the same time, I needed to know. If I was going to be having sex with Damon again, I had to know exactly what I was getting into. It would no longer be a one-night or two-night stand. We would be fuck buddies or even friends with benefits. I had to have a rough idea of what I was stepping into.

"Can I ask ye a question?"

"Generally," Zander said as he flopped down on the other end of the couch.

"When you spoke about Captain Amaro, you seemed to be holdin' back. There seems to be a story there and I was just curious as to what it was."

"It's not really my story to tell," he started, looking down at his lap, and I could tell he was hesitant to let me in. I was getting the feeling though, that it was more public knowledge than something he was trying to keep secret.

"I know and I wouldn't be askin' if I didn't think I needed to know. At the bar, folks seemed to be more interested in keepin' away from him. I'm not lookin' to step on any toes, lad, but I'm also not lookin' to shoot myself in the foot either."

I was really hoping he would tell me. I didn't want to have to go and ask someone else. I didn't want it getting back to Damon that I was asking around about him. I usually wouldn't care, but I couldn't get over this nagging feeling in the pit of my stomach that I needed to know this piece of information. I just needed someone to tell me.

I knew I could have just asked Damon directly, but I seriously doubted he would tell me. He wasn't into sharing, and he had no reason to share with me. I was a twenty-one year old Probee and he was in his late thirties and a Captain. There clearly was a chain of command and my ass was all the way down on the bottom. Professionally and personally, he had no reason to tell me.

Zander let out a soft sigh before he looked around to make sure we were still alone before he spoke. "Captain Amaro has an older brother. Taye. He was a lieutenant with the Fire Department. I didn't know him personally, but Cap had worked with him before he was promoted and transferred here. From what I've heard from different guys, Taye was always weird. There was just something about him that made a lot of people not like him and prefer to avoid him whenever possible. They respected him though, because they are legacies. Their father and grandfather were firefighters and had impressive, records and saves, to say the least. They were legends, so when Taye and Captain

Amaro were eighteen, it was assumed they too, would be enrolled in the Fire Academy. Captain Amaro went into investigations straight from the academy and Taye became a Probee."

I didn't know that Damon was a legacy.

I should have heard about that in the fire academy, so why didn't I?

I had heard the story of other legacies and legendary firefighters; there was a whole class on it, on the history of firefighters. Damon should have been mentioned, or at least his family name. He also should have had his name on the plaques that were at the main entrance to the academy. And I knew it wasn't. I had read every name on those plaques every single morning as I walked through those doors. It was my way of staying motivated and to remind myself what I was fighting for. I wanted to be on one of those plaques one day. The name Amaro never appeared.

"Three months ago, there was an investigation into a series of arsons. They went back twenty-five years and Investigator Tristan Cole, he's the guy that Hawke is dating, discovered that it was the work of two arsonists, a mentor and an apprentice. The mentor found his apprentice ten years ago, roughly, and started to teach him his best practices. Once the apprentice was ready, the mentor stood back and watched the apprentice start the fires. They used cameras to record the whole thing and they would watch them, it's how the mentor was able to get his rocks off still. The investigation revealed that the mentor was an old firefighter who was injured on duty and given a disability pension. Wilson Stan. The apprentice though, was Taye. When Tristan and Detective West went to speak with him, Wilson was there and knocked Detective West out. Taye then tied Tristan to a chair, killed Wilson, and started a fire. We were able to get there in time to save Taye, Tristan, and Detective West. Taye was fine and Detective West and Tristan had some recovering to do, but they are fine now. Now, Taye's kill count is up to forty-eight and he's been connected to twenty-seven fires and that's just so far."

Holy shit.

I was expecting something bad, but I wasn't expecting anything like that. I thought maybe he had done something questionable to someone in the Upper

Brass, had a disagreement about something. I wasn't expecting for his older brother to be an arsonist.

A rather brutal one at that, based on the kill count.

Plus he tried to kill someone who worked underneath Damon.

Shit.

No wonder his family's name wasn't on the plaques, they must have removed them. The Upper Brass would have had to do damage control and the best way to do that would be to erase any traces of the Amaro name. I couldn't help but wonder if they were gunning for Damon next. If he was the last Amaro in the department, they get him out and then they could pretend that the name Amaro never existed.

They had already removed his name

from the curriculum at the academy, obviously. They were teaching the next generation nothing about them and eventually, once the old timers were gone, all that would be left were the young guys who had never heard of the name Amaro. It wasn't fair, but the Upper Brass rarely was.

"I don't even know what to say to that. Do people blame him?" I really hoped not, it wasn't his fault. He shouldn't be held accountable for the actions of his brother.

"Naw. Things are a bit tense between the fire department and the police. Detective West did the right thing by arresting Taye, but that doesn't change that he was a brother and the firefighter brotherhood is pretty strong. Things have also been tense for Tristan. He was investigating not one, but two firefighters and now one has been arrested and the other killed. It's a mess on all fronts. The trial will be starting soon and hopefully, once all of the evidence comes out, people will see that Tristan and Detective West did the right thing. With any luck, they will give Captain Amaro a break. We all know that he didn't have anything to do with it. He had no idea that Taye was even an arsonist. They hadn't spoken in almost a decade. Still, people are doubting it and I'm sure he's getting shit from the Upper Brass about it."

"That explains why everyone was avoidin' him. Still, it's not his fault his own brother did those things. It's not fair to punish a whole family for the actions of one."

The information I'd just learned, and

the fact Damon was pretty much being punished for guilt by association to his brother, was making me even more worried about my own family heritage getting out.

Would they want to kick me out if they discovered my father was one of the most prolific arsonists in Louisiana?

How would they treat me when they discovered that my father was responsible for the death of thirteen firefighters who were killed trying to put out the fires he started?

The information had only solidified what I suspected all along, no one could know my heritage or anything about my past or everything I had worked for would be ruined.

Our conversation was interrupted by the alarm going off. A house fire roughly ten blocks away, according to the dispatch announcement. We both climbed to our feet and trotted off to grab our gear and suit up.

It was going to be my first official fire and I was bouncing with excitement. At least internally. It was wrong to be excited about a house fire, I knew that. There could be people trapped in the house and in danger. I had no business being excited. However, I was only keyed up about getting to help put out a real fire. It was different when it was happening for real and it wasn't just a drill in a burn house.

It didn't take long before we arrived at the scene of the call. I could just make out the house from the window and it didn't look too bad. There weren't any flames coming from the windows and the roof was still intact. It looked like we might have arrived in time to save the house. We climbed out of the truck and Cap instantly started to call out orders.

"Sinclair, take a hose with the rookie and do the primary line inside."

"Sure thing, Cap. Let's go Probee!" Sinclair called out to me.

I was actually getting to be on the primary line, this was awesome! Based on how I was kept off to the side as an observer for the accidents, I'd had a feeling I would be on the fire hydrant or something. I didn't think I would actually get to be in the house and working the hose.

I ran over to help Sinclair with pulling the hose out and we made out way into the house while Gage hooked it up to the hydrant. The second we walked in, I could see where the fire was coming from. The kitchen. It hadn't overtaken the house, but the whole kitchen was on fire and it was spreading across the floor, rapidly making its way to the living room. We had arrived just in time. Another five minutes and the first floor would have been a goner.

Fire didn't take nearly as long as people suspected to spread, especially in a house filled with furniture and curtains. A lot of household furniture and objects could be accelerants if it was hot enough. Manufacturers could only make fabric fire resistant to a certain level and it was never enough to protect it from a hot burning fire. This fire was burning hot from the stove. I could make out a pot on the stove and I was willing to bet the homeowner had been cooking something and grease dropped down into the open fire from the gas burner. It happened more times than people thought and it was often the cause for the majority of kitchen fires.

"All right, Probee, you're taking the nozzle. You're gonna hold it tight, just like in the academy. You aim it low to cut off the fuel to the fire."

"Aye, Lieutenant," I said as I took the hose from him.

Sinclair went behind me and held onto the hose to help me control the flow. The power that flooded through the hose was always immense and it took a lot of physical strength to be able to keep control of the hose and where the water was hitting the fire.

I made sure I had a strong grip on it before I pulled the release valve on the nozzle and the water came shooting out of it. I aimed it low. Most would assume you aim it high so the water sprays down onto the fire. However, you have to aim the water low because that is where all of the fuel and oxygen for the fire comes from. The water chokes off that fuel and oxygen and it kills the fire from the base, eliminating the flames that are attached to it.

Getting to put out a real fire for the first time felt indescribable. I was getting to be a real firefighter and I felt like I was on the moon. The adrenaline high was likely to last me hours.

It took a good ten minutes before the flames had died down and I was able to put the fire out. I couldn't get the smile off of my face. I had put out an actual fire. I had saved someone's house. Today had just started and it was already one of the best days of my life. This was why I had chosen to become a firefighter over anything else. To be able to help people, to save lives, and to save homes. Today was only going to get better. I just knew it.

CHAPTER SEVEN

Damon

IT HAD BEEN a week since I had last seen Cy. I hadn't texted him, because I wanted the anticipation to build up. I wanted him to wonder if I was going to text him. I wanted him to have to wait longer before he could come, assuming he listened to my order. I wouldn't know until I saw him again in person and asked. I would know if he was lying to me based on his facial expression when he answered the question.

I was hoping he had listened, that he was willing to play along. He seemed more than willing that night at the factory. There was no doubt in my mind that he had Daddy issues and that should have been a red flag for me. That meant he had emotional issues and baggage and wouldn't be someone who would be able to handle a no-strings attached relationship like the one I would be interested in.

I didn't want a relationship with emotions and obligations. I didn't want strings. I wanted to be free to come and go whenever I wanted and had control of everything. It wasn't easy for a man to give up control to a complete stranger.

They wanted to know the other guy first and build up trust. It was that very reason why I didn't have relationships. I didn't want anyone to get to know me.

Once they got to know you, they thought they had a say in your life. They started to make demands like meeting my family or my friends. They demanded that I come out of the closet and when I told them no, they assumed it was because I didn't care about them. It was just easier to avoid all of that and I was really hoping that Cy would follow the rules and be a good boy. If not, then I would forget about him and move on to someone who would.

There was a knock at my door and I let out a sigh. I wasn't in the mood to deal with people. That's why I kept my door shut, after all, so I wouldn't have to be bothered. Apparently, whoever was on the other side didn't get the memo.

I needed to get out of here. I needed a stiff drink and some fun. I had already been thinking about texting Cy and having him come over tonight. I didn't need to get a hotel room, not if I was going to be having an ongoing fling with him.

I didn't tend to bring anyone back to my condo, but I didn't know where Cy lived and it was safer to have him come to me than for me to go to him. If he lived in a highly populated area, I couldn't risk being seen by someone who might recognize me going into his place. I also didn't know if he lived alone.

When there was another knock, I knew whoever was on the other side wasn't going away, which meant they knew I was in here. Forcing myself to sit up straight in my chair and pick up a pen so it looked like I was busy doing paperwork, I called out.

"Enter."

My door opened and on the other side was a man I didn't recognize. He wasn't dressed like anyone from the Upper Brass in his suit and I knew the suit was too expensive for him to be a fire investigator that I hadn't met personally. I didn't know what he wanted, but the briefcase in his hand told me he was here on business and I suspected I wasn't going to like the business he had with me.

"Can I help you?" I asked, doing my best to keep the annoyance out of my voice. Some days though, were harder than others.

"My name is Kevin Fox and I am your brother's defense attorney. I have been trying to get a hold of you for months now."

Fuck.

This man was one of the last people I wanted to speak with. The only one above him would be my brother. He had been calling me for months, since the morning he received my brother's case, in fact.

I had no idea why he had agreed to be my brother's lawyer. I knew Taye didn't have money, for one, not with the cops freezing his accounts after he tried to kill one of their own. Cops were generally good people, but if you tried to harm one of their own, if you killed or almost killed one of their own, they were relentless and they would destroy you. They had frozen every asset and bank account that Taye had before dawn the following day. They had destroyed what was left of his house and they investigated for evidence. They went to his locker at the firehouse and took everything from it. They impounded his car and even reached out to the insurance company that had his 401K and made sure no funds were allowed to leave it.

Taye was going to be stuck with a legal aid lawyer who worked for a salary and not by the hour. The result was a bunch of overworked attorneys that didn't really care if they got you out of prison or not.

I had been happy that Taye would get a shitty lawyer because I was hoping that meant he would be forced to take a plea deal. I didn't want to have to go through a trial. I didn't want Tristan to have to go through a trial. It was bad enough that he had been through something traumatic; he shouldn't have to relive it all over again with the hope that a jury would find Taye guilty.

I had no doubt though, that they would find him guilty. There was no way he was getting off from any of it. Even if they couldn't convict him for the fires, he had killed Wilson in front of Tristan and then proceeded to try and kill him and Detective West. He was done. He was going to prison for life just off of that one incident.

"I have nothing to say to you about Taye. I don't care about whatever message he is trying to get you to relay. If that's all, you can leave."

Kevin pulled out a folded up piece of

paper from his inside suit pocket and handed it over to me. I took it as he spoke.

"I am calling you as a witness on your brother's behalf. This is a subpoena to appear in court once the trial starts in thirty days. Have a good day, Captain," he said, before he turned and headed out, closing the door behind him.

"What the fuck?"

I opened the subpoena and saw that he wanted me to testify on Taye's behalf, but it didn't specify what exactly I would be testifying to. I wasn't there during the attack, so I couldn't speak to what happened. I could only talk about what Tristan had told me while he was working the case.

Barba had said that there was a chance he would have to call me, but I would just be testifying to the case itself and what I had recommended for Tristan to do. And that was only if he needed that deep of a background history on the case, something he doubted he needed.

This subpoena, the demand to show up in court and testify on behalf of my brother, was confusing and shocking. I wasn't certain how I felt about it outside of confusion.

I was also surprised that the trial was going to start in thirty days. I thought for sure Taye would take a plea deal to get less prison time. I didn't think he would want to drag it all out through a trial.

I picked up my desk phone and called Barba. I had to find out what was going on. I hadn't spoken to him except that one time when he told me I might have to testify. I hadn't asked about the case;

I didn't want to know. I didn't want to get involved. I wanted to forget that any of it was going on and be kept in the background of it all.

After four rings, Barba answered and he sounded exhausted and overworked.

"ADA Barba."

"Joseph, It's Damon Amaro. You got a minute to talk?"

I knew he was busy and I didn't know if he was about to head into court. I was hoping he would have a minute so I could get to the bottom of this shit without having to wonder about it for the rest of the day.

"I'm assuming this is about the subpoena you just got from Taye's lawyer."

"You knew it was coming? I would have appreciated a heads up."

"Just found out this morning. Fox has been working on trying to get your brother's name cleared. He has filed a plea of not guilty due to mental impairment."

"What? He's not mentally impaired." I rolled my eyes at that news. I seriously couldn't believe Taye was trying to get off with that bullshit excuse for what he had done. Of course he wasn't going to be a man and take his punishment like he deserved. Of course he wasn't going to do what was right and make things easier for everyone. Nope, he wanted to drag our family's name through the mud even more with a public trial and now he wanted to make it seem like it wasn't his fault.

This was so much bullshit.

"Fox is trying to show that the

emotional and mental abuse he suffered as a child has permanently altered his mind and has given him PTSD that was made worse by being a firefighter. He wants to make it appear that Stan manipulated him during a vulnerable time when his father was killed in a fire that Stan started. He's going to attempt to make it appear that Taye had been abused his whole life and is a victim and shouldn't be held accountable for the fires that Stan forced him to start."

Unbelievable.

It was all a load of shit. He didn't have PTSD. He wasn't affected by our father growing up. They spent the most of their time together. He had been a firebug since he was a young child. He was born that way. He wasn't made into a monster by how he grew up.

"That's complete shit. He started a fire when he was a kid. He's always been like this. He kept a scrapbook of the worst fires he had come across in his career and he used to look at them before he went to sleep at night. He loved the gruesome fires. He's not scarred, he's just fucked up."

"I agree and I think Fox looking to call you to the stand is going to destroy his case completely. That doesn't mean he's not going to turn it into a complete circus first. He took Taye's case pro bono. He is already working the press. He wants to make this into a huge show. With the number of fires that Taye started and the deaths and injuries connected to them, it's huge news. Stan and Taye are the first partner arsonists in decades and the press is chomping at the bit to get coverage on it.”

“Great, so Fox is just looking to build his own exposure. Tell me this isn’t going to work.”

The last thing I was going to be able to handle was Taye getting off on all of it. I knew if he was found not guilty due to mental impairment, he still wouldn’t be able to be a firefighter, but that wouldn’t stop him from starting fires again. It wouldn’t put him in a mental institution. He would be a free man to do whatever he wanted.

“Not a chance. It’s going to blow up in his face. You are not a mess. You are not starting fires just to deal with the pressure your father put on you. He can’t claim that the home you both grew up in permanently damaged Taye when you are perfectly fine. If he was an only child or if you were in prison for starting fires or killing people, then he might have had a chance, but you aren't so he doesn't have one. It's just a reason for him to drag it all out. I have offered a plea deal, but Fox refuses to allow Taye to accept it. He's got Taye believing he can get away with it all. Realistically, with the number of homicides through the fires, he's looking at the death penalty. A plea deal would take that off the table, and Taye knows that, but he's refusing to cooperate."

I could hear that Barba was frustrated by the entire situation, too. He had probably figured that this case would be easy enough to plead out. Most criminals would take a plea deal if it meant they wouldn't get the death penalty, but of course Taye wasn't going to do things the easy way. Arsonists loved the limelight and he was thriving on the thought of all the attention he would be getting from a public trial.

"And someone who almost killed a cop is treated like a God in prison. It's not like he has any motivation on the inside to get a deal. He's probably got prisoners kissing his feet. What if I don't testify?"

"You've been served, you don't have a choice. If you don't show up, you can be arrested for contempt of court, and then still have to testify but Fox will treat you like a hostile witness. He'll get you on that stand one way or the other, so it would be better for you to testify and not have to spend two days in lock up for contempt of court. The best thing you can do is show up and tell the truth. He will get to question you first and then I will, so if there is something that is a little gray, we can clear it up on my cross."

"Yeah, all right." I rubbed my hand over my face, still shaking my head over the whole situation.

I wasn't happy about it, but there was nothing that I could do about, it either. I was going to be testifying whether I wanted to or not. I might as well do it the easy way.

We said our goodbyes and I debated for a moment before I gave in and pulled my cell phone out. I knew that it was going to be a terrible idea, but I needed something to put me in a better mood. I needed some type of a release and I might as well make it good. I hit Will's contact number and put it to my ear and listened to the rings. After three of them he finally answered.

"Hey, D, how the hell are ya?"

"I'm fine, just busy over here. I need you to send over your new Probee to my office."

"Is something wrong?" he asked, and I could hear his concern that Cy had screwed something up or was being investigated for something.

"Naw, the Upper Brass has us walking all of the new Probees through the division and offer tips on how they can better identify arson. I just need him for a few minutes, then he'll be back with you."

"Yeah, okay. I'll let him know and send him your way. I'm sure the Upper Brass are looking to cover their asses with everything that is going on. You want to talk about it yet?"

I could hear the concern in his voice and I didn't blame him for it. Will knew I was struggling, but doing so silently. I wasn't ready to open up to anyone right now about all of this shit with Taye. What I wanted was for Cy to get over here and suck my dick. Talking could come later.

"Nope. I'll see you later. Be safe."

"You, too."

I ended the call and tossed my cell phone down onto my desk before I sat back in my chair. Soon, Cy would be here and he would be able to take the edge off. I wasn't going to let him come, not yet. That would be tonight. I was going to make sure he was craving my touch all day long. Now, I just needed him here and the fun could start.

CHAPTER EIGHT

Cyrus

I KNOCKED ON Damon's office door and waited until I was told I could enter. I was surprised when Cap told me that Damon had asked for me to go down. Apparently, the Upper Brass wanted all of the new guys to see early and obvious signs of arson. I wasn't sure I believed that was why I was being asked to come down here, though. At least, I was hoping that wasn't why.

I highly doubted that Damon brought me down here so we could have sex in his office, either. That would be very bold, especially for a man who I suspected wasn't out of the closet yet.

Still, a man can dream right?

"Enter," Damon called out.

I could tell by the tone in his voice that he was stressed and not happy. I couldn't help but wonder if it had something to do with his brother. It still blew my mind about all of it. To know that his own brother had done something like that, most people wouldn't understand how he was feeling, but I did. I went through the very same emotions with my father and I could completely understand what he was feeling. It made sense why he was taking a stronger control in the bedroom. Why he would be drinking and getting drunk during the week. He didn't start those fires. He didn't kill those people, but he would feel the guilt all the same.

I knew that Taye wouldn't be capable of feeling guilt, my father sure as shit doesn't. But I did. I felt the guilt of every life that my father took. Damon would be feeling that same guilt and there was nothing that anyone could do or say that would make it magically disappear. I was still dealing with it and what my father had done happened years ago. All of this was still fresh for Damon and it truly made sense for him to be spiraling slightly.

I strolled into his office and saw that he was sitting at his desk with a bunch of paperwork scattered around it. He glanced up for a moment before he leaned back in his chair and looked me up and down. A shiver of excitement ran down my spine with the way he looked at me. There was just something about this man.

"Close the door," he ordered.

I closed the door behind me and waited to see what he wanted to talk about. I didn't care what it was that he wanted, I was more than happy to spend the rest of my day here just looking at him.

This past week had been brutal. I'd spent it fighting with my dick to not get hard while at work and fighting to get my dick soft while I was out of work. I'd spent all night long hard just thinking about sex with Damon.

I knew I could have touched myself, but he had told me not to and I couldn't bring myself to go against him. Every night, I went to sleep my dick was hard. Every morning, I woke up to a hard and aching dick, but I never touched myself. I never allowed myself to come, just like I had been told. I was in a constant state of blue balls at this point, but I would be lying if I said I didn't enjoy this game we were playing.

"Get down on your knees and crawl over here to suck Daddy's cock," he ordered, and my dick instantly went hard.

Holy fuck.

We were actually going to do this right here in his office. Anyone could come in; anyone could hear us. I thought he was in the closet, but apparently that closet door wasn't as tightly nailed shut as I thought it was.

This was insane.

We could get caught.

This could ruin my career as a firefighter and yet, I slid down on my hands and knees and started to crawl toward him. I went around his desk as he turned in his chair and opened his pants, pulling out his hard cock for me. My mouth watered at the sight of the already engorged flesh, his tip glistening with precum.

My own cock was hard and already pulsing with need. I was praying that after getting him off he was going to finally let me come. The second I was close enough, his hand went into my hair, pulling on it tight as he pushed my head down on his cock. I relaxed my throat as he pushed my head all the way down to his base.

I moaned as I felt his cock sliding down my throat. I'd missed him. I'd missed his dick and how it could make me feel, how good it felt in my mouth and down my throat.

"Rub your cock on the outside of your pants, but stop when you are going to come. You are not allowed to come yet, my slut."

A deep moan escaped my mouth at his words. I instantly did as I was told and started slowly rubbing my cock along its length through my pants. I was insanely hard and all I wanted to do was to come. I was going to be a good boy though, and then he should allow me to come. I knew I was still being punished for coming without permission from last time and I was not about to make that same mistake twice.

I couldn't stop moaning and humming my appreciation as he started to fuck my mouth. I knew I had to be careful, I didn't want anyone to overhear us, but with his cock in my mouth my moans were muffled.

He was more aggressive this time with his thrusts, but I suspected he was in just as much of a need to orgasm as I was. I also suspected that something had pissed him off enough to bring me here. The man was in the closet and this was a very bold move for him to be making. He was clearly in desperate need of a release, but he wasn't the only one. I had to stop my hand and squeeze my cock through my pants to stop myself from coming. With my pleasure denied, my balls got even heavier.

"Good boy. That's my good slut," he praised, and it only turned me on even more.

He picked up his pace and I knew he was chasing his own release. I suspected that my throat was going to be a bit sore after this, but I didn't care, it was well worth it.

His grunts were soft and I knew if I looked up he would be biting his lip to keep his groans inside. I knew he was close, I could feel his cock getting harder, swelling against my tongue.

After a few more thrusts of his hips, he pushed my head down fully on his cock as he shoved his hips up, forcing his cock as deep as possible down my throat as he came with a deep groan, his grip tightening in my hair and sending shivers down my spine. I greedily swallowed his cum as he continued to pulse in my throat. I would never get tired of this feeling. I could have done this all day without a single complaint.

He pulled my head back once I finished swallowing everything he had for me. He placed his right hand underneath my jawline and pulled me in for a rough kiss. I easily melted against him and opened my mouth when I felt his tongue seeking entrance. I moaned at the roughness, as he took control over me. He knew how to make me writhe and whimper beneath him and I relished every moment of his control.

All too soon he was pulling back, but he kept his hand on my throat. He stood, pulling me up with him, and then he quickly turned me around so I was facing his desk.

"Drop your pants and bend over, my slut."

"Aye, Daddy."

I was more than happy to drop my pants. I was painfully hard and desperately needed to come. I needed to feel his cock buried deep inside of my ass. I didn't care anymore that we were still in his office and anyone could overhear us or walk in on us. The need to come, the need to feel him inside of me, was stronger than any logic running through my mind.

He placed his hand on my back and pushed me forward. I laid my chest flat against his cool desk without complaint or resistance as he spoke.

"Spread your ass. Show your Daddy that sweet hole."

I moaned as I reached behind me and spread my ass cheeks apart for him. My dick pulsed and I knew if he touched me, I was going to explode. My balls were heavy and aching with the need for release.

"Daddy has something for his little slut," he growled into my ear. He was so close I could feel his hard cock pressing against my needy hole.

"Oh fuck. Aye, Daddy," I whined.

I heard him opening his desk drawer and I was praying it was for lube. I didn't want to know why he had it in his office, and I didn't care right now. All that mattered at that moment was him pounding into me.

When I finally felt something against my hole, it wasn't a lubed up finger. It wasn't even his tip; this wasn't flesh against my hole, it was silicone. I knew that feeling all too well.

I had to bite my lip to keep the deep groan from echoing off the walls as he pushed in the butt plug. It wasn't too big, but it was big enough to sting as it was slowly pushed inside of me. I had no idea how long it was, but it was longer than the last one I had in me. When I felt the blunt end rub up against my prostate before he finally bottomed out, I couldn't help but shudder. It was long enough that it would constantly rub up against my sweet spot with every step I took. If I sat down, I was going to be feeling it.

I was not shy when it came to sex toys. I had used plenty of butt plugs and dildos in my life. I had a healthy sex drive and when I couldn't hook up with a guy I had no problem pleasuring myself.

"Get dressed," he demanded.

"What?" I asked, shocked.

He didn't just tell me get dressed, that didn't happen.

That can't happen.

I can't get dressed.

I had a raging hard-on, and I had this toy up my ass. I needed to *come*. I needed him to let me come or make me come. I did not need my pants back on.

"Get dressed, slut. Don't make me repeat myself," he said with a deadly edge to his voice.

"Sorry, Daddy," I instantly said. The last thing I wanted was for him to not let me come again.

I stood up and pulled my boxers and pants back up. It was not easy with the plug inside of me. I could handle a larger one, but usually I wasn't going to be walking around with it.

Once I was dressed, he turned me around and started to rub his hand along my hard cock through my pants as he spoke.

"There are rules you will have to follow if you want to keep doing this."

"What rules, Daddy?" I knew there would be, but I wasn't certain what all of them would be. To be honest though, at that point, I so didn't fucking care what they were as long as it ended up with me coming.

"I am in control of everything sexual between us. You come only when I give you permission to. This never gets talked about with anyone. I am not out and I do not plan on ever being out. As far as anyone will ever know, you're just another Rookie and I'm a highly respected Captain. Are you negative?"

"Aye." I didn't need him to elaborate more on what he meant.

"Good, so am I. Moving forward there won't be condoms. When I am fucking you, I will be coming deep inside of your needy ass and I will own you. Your body will belong to me. Neither one of us will be with anyone else. There won't be any dates, going out. When we are in public, I won't even acknowledge you unless it is for professional reasons. You are nothing more than a dirty needy slut for me to put my cock into. Now, is that something that you can agree to?"

The answer should be, no. No, I didn't agree to be a living sex doll for him to use whenever he felt like it. But I also knew that human beings were stupid.

CYRUS

I was stupid.

If I was smart and made smart choices, I never would have slept with my teacher. I never would have gone to sex parties as an underage kid. I am not that smart, not when it came to sex and my body. I knew all of that. I knew I should say no. He was essentially telling me I was going to be his personal prostitute, only I wouldn't get paid for anything he did to me. I was also going to have to go through it knowing that there was a chance he wouldn't let me come every time, meaning I got nothing out of our time together. Even though I knew all of that, every ounce, every fiber in my being, was screaming at me to say *yes*.

I was clearly a glutton for punishment. I really needed to consider speaking to a Shrink about my issues and obvious lack of self-esteem if I was even considering agreeing to his demands. Even knowing exactly what he wanted from me. Even knowing that I was never going to be anything more than a dirty secret—shit, a dirty secret would be a step up to what this would be. Still, even knowing all of that, there really was only one answer I could give.

"I can agree to your terms, Daddy."

Maybe I would live to regret it, but that was my choice to make. I could also live to regret not agreeing to it and allowing this opportunity to pass me by. If I was going to regret something, I would rather regret doing something then not doing anything.

"That's my good slut. I will text you my address. When you are done work tonight, you will drive there. When you arrive, you will text me and then wait until I text you back to give you permission to come up. Do you understand?"

"Aye, Daddy. I'll be your good slut and do as I'm told."

"Good, now get out of my office," he said as he moved back.

"Aye," I said as I started to move away.

With every step I took, I noticed the toy up my ass. It was going to take some getting used to and it was going to be hard when a call came in. I was only just two hours into my shift and I had ten more to go.

This was going to be a long ass day.

Just as I opened the door, I was thrown through another shock. There was a man standing on the other side of it and he was clearly about to knock on the door. The second his gaze landed on me, he instantly registered who I was and disgust quickly grew upon his face. Before he had a chance to say anything, I was moving and quickly making my escape.

Ronnie Mack.

Fire Investigator Ronnie Mack. The man who had been responsible for discovering my father was a serial arsonist.

I can still remember clearly the night he stormed into our home and dragged my father out in cuffs. He didn't even care that I was there. That I was mourning the loss of my mother. He just threw my father down and cuffed him, going on and on about all the people he'd killed, including my mother.

Then, he tossed me into another police car and dragged me down to the station and put me in an interrogation room. I was in there for over twelve hours, not being spoken to, never checked on, no food, no water, not even a bathroom break.

When he finally did come in, it was to interrogate me to make sure I wasn't starting fires with my old man. They held me for a total of forty-eight hours before they let me go. Twenty in that interrogation room with no food, water or a bathroom break, even when I did ask. I spent the rest of it in a holding cell with other adult males, some of which gave me extra special attention when I finally did get to use the toilet in the cell. Only to be let go two days later and into the custody of social services. By then, my mother had been buried and no one knew where. It took six months before my lazy ass worker finally told me where she was.

I understood that Mack had a job. I understood that my father was a criminal, a murderer, a mass murderer by all accounts. I got that. What I didn't understand still to this day was how anyone could treat me like he did. I was just a kid. I didn't deserve to be treated like a killer. I didn't deserve to be treated like I was worthless and some criminal that they could do whatever they wanted with.

I'd had no idea he was even still working. I figured he would have retired by now. He was older to begin with back then, in his early sixties. After that arrest, he should have retired and gone out on an epic high note. If he was still working that meant that Damon was his Captain. There was no way Mack wasn't going to be telling Damon all about me and my father.

A deep sadness overtook me at the knowledge that Mack was going to tell Damon. That Damon was going to hear about how my father was a prolific serial arsonist and I was hauled in for questioning on the crimes. That he always suspected I'd helped, but he could never prove it. Mack had taken something from me growing up when he arrested me and now he was going to take my career and someone that could possibly be a long-time lover.

Someone who I could possibly fall in love with one day.

He was going to ruin my life and once again, there was nothing that I could do to stop it. He had made me powerless again.

I got into my car and started to head back to the firehouse for what very well could be my last shift as a firefighter.

CHAPTER NINE

Damon

IT WAS CLOSER to eleven when I finally decided to text Cy and let him know he was allowed to come up. I knew I was being more controlling than I usually would and I knew there was only so long it would be fun and exciting for Cy before he got sick of it and wanted some control and equality in this arrangement.

It was only logical and rational for Cy to grow tired of being treated like a piece of meat. At first it was always fun and exciting, but it took a toll on a person's mind and I knew he wouldn't last for very long. He was young and had his whole life ahead of him. The world wasn't all darkness and horror to him yet. He could still see the sunlight, something I used to be able to see before everything went to shit. I couldn't let this go on for very long. I didn't want my darkness to taint his light. He was still young, he had a lot of years left to live, and the last thing I wanted to do was for him to see the world as nothing but shades of darkness. That wouldn't be fair to him. We could have some fun for a bit and then I had to let him go, no matter what.

I was pulled out of my thoughts at the knock on my door. I knew it was Cy and I knew he was going to be in serious need of coming. I might have been taking things too far with him. Normally, I would never have him wearing a plug that size for that long and never at work. I had gotten too excited and let my lust cloud my thinking. It was something I would be more cautious with in the future and I would be speaking to him about it and letting him know I was crossing a line. That would come after, though.

Sex first and then talking.

I opened the door and I could see how desperate he was, it was written all over his face. I felt a wave of pride hit me at knowing how crazy I could drive this young twenty-one year old man. He was well on his way to craving my touch and it was only going to get worse after tonight.

"Follow," I ordered, before turning around. I heard his quick and eager footsteps behind me as he closed my front door. Tonight was going to be exactly what we both needed and I couldn't wait.

We walked into my bedroom and I could see the surprise and excitement mixed within his eyes. I had four restraints already set up on my bed and he didn't need me to tell him that they were for him. I was going to have him tied down and at my complete mercy. Tonight, he was going to finally get to come and I was going to make sure I milked him for every last drop he had been building up over the past week.

***

With the last restraint removed from Cy, his body instantly collapsed down onto my bed. I could see him struggling to catch his breath and I knew he was thoroughly pleased. He had come six times and I was surprised he even had any left after the first five of them. I knew I had made up for the wait though, and it pleased me to see him so sated he was practically jelly.

"You all right?" I asked, flashing him a knowing smirk.

"Aye," he said in a dreamy voice, and I knew he was well up on cloud nine right now.

"Look, I'm sorry about earlier with the plug. I was out of line having that in you while you were going to work. I got a bit carried away and I'm sorry if it distracted you while you were at work or made the guys look at you like something was wrong."

It really wasn't fair of me to do that to him. I knew better, but I had been so blinded by my own lust that I unintentionally put him in harm's way while he was working. I also put him in a position for the guys he works with to think something was going on with him.

"The guys didn't notice and you have nothing to be sorry for. That was fun. Maybe not with one that long again, bit awkward to sit down for very long, other than that it was good. I enjoy using toys and having a plug in me during the day or at night. I like the feeling. I like feeling like I'm connected to someone and not alone. I enjoyed today and I'm hoping to do it again, Daddy," he said, flashing me a sexy smirk and a wink. It sent a heatwave all through my body.

Fuck, this man just might be perfect.

Too bad I was not interested in having a relationship.

Even if I was, could I really have one with a twenty-one year old?

We were at two completely different points in our lives, in our careers. He would want to go out and party at his age and I was past the club-hopping phase. There was also a maturity level difference. Most twenty-one year olds were irresponsible and immature. It wasn't their fault, they were still growing up and learning who they were. We'd all done it. I was just past that stage in my life.

Now I was in a new stage of my life, my early mid-life crisis where I drank, did drugs, and had random sex with strangers.

Shit, maybe we were at the same maturity level.

He pushed himself up and started to get dressed. I knew we weren't going to be going around again, we were both spent and it was getting late. He had to be at work tomorrow morning at eight.

"The man who went into your office when I left, did he say anything about me?" he asked, carefully, and I was surprised by the wave of jealousy that hit me.

"I was serious about the rule 'you don't fuck with anyone else,'" I responded with a slight growl to my voice.

"Don't make me yak. He's old enough to be my Grandda."

"And I'm old enough to be your father if I started young. He didn't say anything about you, why?"

If he wasn't interested in hooking up with Mack, then why would he want to know if Mack said something about him?

That would lead me to believe that he knew Mack; that they knew each other. Where they would have met I had no idea, perhaps the Fire Academy, but to my knowledge Mack had never volunteered his time there.

Mack was one of my oldest investigators. The man was sixty-seven and should have long retired by now. It wasn't because he loved his job that he was still working. It also wasn't because he needed the money. It had everything to do with he didn't know what else to do. It was not uncommon for firefighters, or first responders in general, to stay well past their retirement age. For most, it was the only life they'd known, the only career they had ever done. They had no wives, only ex-wives, and the ones that did have children, their children hated them or their ex-wives were keeping them apart. They had nothing but the job so they stayed, even when they should have left long ago.

Mack was a good investigator, but he was getting sloppy. He was getting caught up on doing things the old fashioned way. It was becoming difficult to trust him with any high profile case or a serial arsonist case. ADA Barba also cringes whenever he has to try and prosecute Mack's cases now. He has the lowest close rating out of all of my investigators, including my rookies. The Upper Brass liked him, so they were letting him stay on, but pretty soon I was going to have no choice but to let him go. I had been thinking about doing it soon while I was still hated by the Upper Brass. After all, it wasn't like they could hate me more than they already did.

"Nothin'," Cy said, trying to dismiss the conversation as he finished dressing. I wasn't about to let him get away with that, though.

"People don't bring up some random guy after sex for no reason. We can do this one of two ways, Cy. You can either be honest with me and tell me why you want to know if Mack was asking about you, or you don't get to come again until you do tell me, and if I find out from him first, which I will come morning, then I'll make it so that you don't come for the next six months. Which road would you like to take, my slut?"

I knew it was wrong for me to order him to tell me something that had nothing to do with sex. I was crossing a line by doing it, but it seemed like something that was important. He wouldn't have asked unless there was an issue and if there was an issue between one of my investigators and a firefighter, then I had to know about it.

There are investigators and firefighters that I couldn't put together because they didn't get along. It might seem childish, but certain personalities just can't work together and sometimes there's a history there. I had a dozen or more female investigators who had dated a firefighter before and when things went south, I had to keep them apart. It wasn't just for professional or personal reasons, but also legal reasons. A defense lawyer would tear the entire case apart and if they got a whiff of a bad break up it turned into a shit show.

Cy let out a sigh as he rubbed his face before he sat down on the end of my bed next to me.

"My father is Jamie McDougal."

"*The* Jamie McDougal?" I asked, trying to keep the shock from my voice.

Everyone in the fire department knew who Jamie McDougal was. It didn't matter if you were an investigator or an active firefighter, we all knew about him. His name went nationwide. He would be going down in history as the most deadly arsonist. He'd been connected to a hundred and ten fires, that we could prove, and had killed eighty-three people. That didn't include all of the other victims who would forever be scarred by the fires he'd started.

I had still been a rookie Captain when McDougal came across my desk. Mack had been working it. I had assigned it to him with being my most senior investigator. I had trusted him to look through the cases and find the arsonist who was responsible.

At the time five years ago, there were over a dozen fires that could be connected to one arsonist from his signature. We didn't know how many fires were connected to him at the time. We didn't find out until after the arrest was made just how many fires he had started. I was confident there were more, but he was no longer disclosing any. Arsonists liked to talk. They liked to relive their fires. However, there were also fires they liked to keep to themselves. Generally, their favorite ones; the ones that were most significant to them. They kept the information on those to themselves for only them to enjoy. We'd never know how many fires he'd truly started.

"Aye," he said softly.

"I didn't know he had a child. Mack never said anything about him having a son. I know your mother was killed in his last fire. I'm sorry, Cy. I had no idea."

There was nothing anywhere that stated McDougal had a son. It should have been in his case file, but for whatever reason Mack had left that out. I also had more questions about why Cy was a firefighter.

His father was a historic arsonist, why would he pick this career out of all of the possibilities?

"Doesn't surprise me. I changed my last name to my Ma's given name when I turned eighteen. Spent the morning on my eighteenth birthday at the Government office. Mack never told you?" he asked, appearing slightly surprised and confused.

"No. Did he know?" If Mack knew about Cy it should have been in the files. There should have been a report about his interview and the Social Worker's report on him and his placement. That was standard for any investigation where children were left behind.

"Aye, he all but arrested me."

"Hold up, what?" I demanded.

Mack would have had no reason to arrest a sixteen year old kid. If he had brought him in, he should have had a child and youth advocate present for any questioning. He would have had to call in Barba to help with the interview in case there was a reason to press charges. That was standard procedure and it was done that way to protect everyone's asses.

"When he stormed in to arrest my father, he brought me in as well. Put me in the back of a cop car and took me down to the station. He left me alone in an interrogation room for twelve hours before he came in. Then spent the next eight drilling me with questions. He kept tellin' me to admit to helpin' my father. It didn't matter how many times I told him that I had nothin' to do with it. He kept me in that room for twenty hours. No food, no water, wouldn't let me go to the bathroom, he just drilled me with questions. Then he tossed me in a holdin' cell with all of these other blokes until the forty-eight hours were up. I spent twenty-eight hours curled up in the far corner tryin' to keep the perverts from touchin' me. When I finally got to leave, he told me we would be seein' each other again. That he knew I was a firebug and he would prove it. I missed my Ma's funeral while I was in that cell. I didn't even know where she was buried for six months."

The hurt within his voice was still raw and it fueled my rage. What happened to him never should have happened. He was a sixteen year old kid. Even if Mack suspected he was involved it never should have been handled like that. He should have had a lawyer and a child advocate present for any questioning. He should have been kept in a holding cell alone or with other juveniles. He never should have been placed in a holding cell with grown men and he never should have been kept for forty-eight hours without a shred of evidence, for fuck's sake.

Yes, we can hold suspects for forty-eight hours without charging them, but we do so only when we have some scrap of evidence that tells us he is our guy. We hold them so we have the time to find more evidence and build a solid case before charging. Keeping them those two days keeps people safe, it is why we do it. We don't do it because we have nothing and just feel like being assholes, which is exactly what Mack obviously did. I would be talking to him about this tomorrow and he would be reprimanded. I wasn't going to be putting up with this shit from anyone, past or present.

"I'm sorry, that never should have happened to you. I'm assuming no one knows about your connection to McDougal."

Thirteen dead firefighters.

It wouldn't go well for Cy if people discovered who his father was. It wouldn't matter that he was just a kid at the time, or that he didn't have a hand in the fires. They wouldn't care. All they would see was his father and they would ice him out. I didn't know if the guys at the Twenty-First would. Will didn't tolerate bullying of any kind for any reason. I also knew that Will wouldn't hold Cy's father's actions against him. However, the second shift Captain lost his son in one of those fires and that would put a serious strain between the two shifts.

"No, I've kept my mouth shut about it. Though, now I suppose it's only a matter of time before it gets out. I didn't expect for Mack to still be workin'. I thought no one would recognize me so there was no need to disclose."

"Mack has no interest in retiring. Why pick this job? You had to have known it wouldn't have gone over well if people discovered your connection to McDougal."

I mean, was he a glutton for

punishment?

It wasn't like his father started only a couple of fires. He was a huge deal. His name wasn't going to go quietly into the night and be forgotten about. Cy had to know this was potential career suicide.

"I didn't know what I wanted to be when I grew up, not like most kids. I didn't have dreams of being anything. Nothin' interested me. And then I started to hear about my father's fires and all of the people he killed and hurt. I thought maybe I could try and make it right. That I could help people and try and make up for all the pain and destruction that my old man put out into the world. I wanted to be a firefighter and help people. To save lives and to stop people like my father from hurting anyone else. And I'm good at it. Maybe his DNA lets me see things differently, I don't know, but I feel like I can read a fire, know what it's thinkin'. That sounds daft, I know, but being a firefighter feels *right*. It feels like this is what I was born to do and I don't want to lose that."

He was a good man, I had to give him that. Most in his position would have done the opposite. They would have avoided the fire department all together. He had every reason to hate the fire department after what he had been put through. And yet, he wanted to keep helping people. He wanted to help save lives and prevent future arsonists from adding to their tally. It was honorable work and it really showed a level of maturity and what type of man he was. He certainly had more depth and layers to him than I was expecting. Than I judged.

"Will, Captain Clarke, he's a good man and he won't let anyone treat you differently because of your father. That isn't to say that other firefighters won't have an issue, but Will won't kick you out. He won't let anyone push you out. He'll protect you and so will his guys. You can still be a firefighter, you just won't be the most popular kid in school."

"I didn't join to be popular. Even if no one likes me, I'm not goin' nowhere. I got my own reasons for joinin' and if no one likes it, that's too bad for them. I'd appreciate you keepin' this between us. I don't need no sympathy or people lookin' at me funny. They don't need to know what I've been through."

"Of course. If anyone gives you a hard time though, when this eventually comes out, let me know. I can't promise anything, but I will look into it and I know your Captain will as well."

I couldn't make him tell me if someone gave him a hard time, but I was hoping he would tell me anyway. This was going to hit eventually, and my money was on sooner rather than later. I just hoped that the guys at the Twenty-First were there for him and didn't turn their backs on him. I knew Will wouldn't allow it, but that didn't mean they had to talk to him and be friendly. There was being professional and then there was being friends. Tomorrow though, I would be speaking with Mack and getting to the bottom of things. I wasn't going to tolerate that kind behavior from anyone, especially someone who had been here longer than dirt. He knew better and he deliberately went against all of our rules and protocols. There was no excuse for any of it and tomorrow he was going to have to answer to me and he better pray that I liked his answers otherwise his ass was out the door. I wasn't going to stand by and let anyone treat Cy like garbage. As a Captain it was my professional responsibility and obligation to make sure everyone was treated fairly. Even if the situation was in the past. Shit like that didn't fly in my house, ever. Not when I could do something about it. Even if I couldn't make it right for Cy, I could at least make sure Mack got what was coming to him and prevent it from happening to anyone else.

I knew my anger over the situation, how Cy had been treated, might be a little over the top at the moment but it was because I took pride in my team and we worked on the straight and narrow, never deviating into behavior like Mack had displayed. If nothing else, I had an image to maintain and uphold for my team.

It had nothing to do with any personal connection that I had with Cy. At least, that's what I was telling myself.

CHAPTER TEN

Cyrus

I WAS FEELING really good today. Last night with Damon had been amazing and I was really hoping we could keep it up. He seemed to be interested in making it a more ongoing thing and I was excited to see where it would take us. I knew there were plenty of obstacles standing in our way and chances were we weren't going to last very long. But, even though I knew all of that, I still wanted to give what we had a shot. Odds were our attraction would burn hot and flame out pretty quickly, but I was going to enjoy every second that I had with him.

After parking, I made my way into the firehouse through the roll up for the trucks. More often than not there were a few guys that were here in the truck bays, but they weren't outside today. I figured they must be in sitting around the kitchen and living area. Generally, when the shift started, they were always there talking and seeing how everyone's time off was. It was a lot like school in that way. When you first get to school you always check in with your friends, even though you just saw them.

I headed into the main area of the firehouse and my heart instantly dropped down to my stomach.

Investigator Mack stood in the middle of the living area and everyone was surrounding him as they listened to what he had to say. I didn't need to know that I had interrupted his speech, nor did I need to be here from the start to know what he was talking about.

No one even recognized or acknowledged me as I made my way quietly into the room. I knew today was going to go downhill with him being here and there would be nothing I could do about any of it now. All I could do was wait until he finished telling my deepest, darkest secret before he waltzed out of here and left me with the destruction.

"He's been going by his mother's

maiden name, but his real last name is McDougal. His father was *Jamie McDougal*, something he must not have disclosed on his application, otherwise they never would have taken him. I had arrested him and I have always believed he was involved in the fires, but there wasn't enough evidence for it to stick. The Department already has a black mark smearing its reputation with Taye Amaro up on multiple murder and arson charges. The last thing we need is another arsonist within our ranks. I have already reported him to the Upper Brass and they will be looking into him, but while that happens, I felt like you all should know."

This arsehole was making me look like an accomplice to multiple counts of arson and murder when I had nothing to do with any of it. I was just a sixteen year old kid and he came into my life and destroyed it. He treated me like I was a murderer, like I had helped to plan those fires and purchased the gasoline myself.

I was just a kid, for god's sake, and as far as I knew my parents had a healthy and happy marriage. I thought my father was a normal and loving father just like everyone else. I saw no signs. I wasn't old enough to know what the signs even were supposed to be. And Investigator Mack was looking to make a bigger name for himself by trying to intimidate and arrest a kid for the crimes of his father.

It made me wonder what his relationship was like with his own father. Maybe that was why he was so bound and bet on ruining my life and reputation. I was just starting my career as a firefighter and I wasn't going to let him destroy it, not while it was within my power.

I didn't have to declare the name change or my connection to my father. They never asked if I had any criminals in my family tree. All they cared about was my own criminal background check and it came back clean. If the Upper Brass had a problem with my genetic connection to my father, then that was too bad. They had no legal reason to terminate me and if they tried, they would be in for the fight of their lives. I was not going to go quietly into the night.

"I appreciate you coming down, Mack, and giving us the head's up," Captain

Clarke said, his face stoic and unreadable.

I didn't know him well enough to know if he was being polite or he genuinely was going to have a problem with me now. Damon had said he wouldn't stand for it, that he would be on my side. I wanted to believe him, but it was hard when I didn't know the Captain all that well just yet.

"It was the least I could do. I would hate to see any of your men being hurt because of him," Investigator Mack said, as he held his hand out to Captain Clarke.

The Captain shook the offered hand with a small smile in return. It was then that Investigator Mack turned around and his gaze finally landed on me.

I had stayed back by the entrance to

the kitchen from the roll up, everyone had been so focused on Mack's words that they hadn't even noticed me coming into the room.

Mack gave me a smirk, and it took everything in me not to punch him right across the jaw as he walked right by me. He knew what he had done and I was praying that he had failed. That the men I had been working beside, even for a short time, knew me better than to think I was an arsonist, especially at the young age of sixteen.

The second we were alone, Captain Clarke spoke first. I was thankful that he had said something, because I wasn't certain I would be able to form any words right now.

"I'm assuming you heard most of that."

"Aye, Captain," I said with a small nod. I had no idea where he was going to go with it, but I was hoping Damon was right and the Captain wouldn't tell me to pack my gear and get out.

"Mack has always been an asshole. The Upper Brass have been trying to figure out a way to get him to retire, but they can't force him and he hasn't done anything worthy of being forced into retirement. I know Damon would love to get rid of him. Is there anything you would like to address about what Mack said?" Captain Clarke finished.

I breathed a sigh of relief at his words. I felt better knowing that the Captain didn't like Mack. I was hoping that meant that he was on my side with all of this. I was going to need all of the support that I could get and it would help to have support from someone with a Captain ranking. I knew I had Damon on my side as well, but I had no idea what was going to happen with our personal relationship and I didn't think it would be wise to assume that if we stopped seeing each other that he would be on my side.

"I didn't know what my father was doing. I didn't have anything to do with it," I started, but Zander cut me off before I could get much further.

"We might not be mathletics, but we can do basic math and know that you would have been sixteen at the time."

"We know you didn't have anything to do with the fires. That's not even up for debate," Sinclair added.

It made me feel good to know that these men knew, without me even having to say it, that I wasn't an arsonist. That I didn't have anything to do with what my father had done. I felt a weight being lifted from my shoulders and I was getting to see a bit of the light at the end of the tunnel just knowing that they believed me.

"I'm assume Mack didn't feel the same though, based on what he just said," Newt said.

"Naw, he didn't. He treated me like a suspect, including putting me with adult males in a holding cell for twenty-eight hours until someone finally came and got me out. My Da killed my Ma in his last fire, that was his mistake. When I got out of that holdin' cell, I was placed in foster care. I didn't even get to go to her funeral," I said.

"He had no right to do that to you.

You were just a kid. I'm assuming you didn't disclose the connection on your Fire Academy application," Captain Clarke asked, understanding in his voice.

"Naw. They didn't ask about any connection to a criminal or arsonist. I had changed my name on my eighteenth birthday to my Ma's maiden name. I didn't see the need to mention who my father was. I think part of me was scared they would turn me away and all I wanted to be was a firefighter."

"Why? Out of all of the things that you could have been, why a firefighter?" Gage asked, obviously not understanding why I would choose to put myself in the situation at all.

"I know it doesn't make sense, that I should want to be anything else. But I wanted to be a firefighter so I could help people. To save lives that might have otherwise been taken by a fire. The lives my father took, those are not on me and I have no business taking on that guilt, but the guilt is there anyway. If I can help people and try and save more lives than the lives he took, that's a peace I can live with."

I wasn't certain how well they would take my answer. I knew that some could argue that my intentions were misguided and I shouldn't be a firefighter with the desire to try and even out the scale left behind by my father. It was the truth though, and it was part of the reason why my desire to be a firefighter was so strong. But I also wanted to be a firefighter because I enjoyed the work. My intentions were pure and hopefully they would see that; if not today then in the near future when I had earned their full trust and respect.

"It's not your guilt to carry, Kid," Sinclair instantly said, his hand going to my shoulder in comfort.

"Aye, I know, but the guilt lives there all the same. I had wanted to be a firefighter for years, so the second I was able to apply, I was first in line. I want this career, I want this life, and I am not about to let anyone keep me from it," I said with strength in my voice.

"And you shouldn't. Mack is an asshole, and he can tell the Upper Brass whatever he wants, at the end of the day you were never arrested or charged and you were a juvenile. It holds no weight over your employment. Even if someone within the Upper Brass wants to make a thing out of this, you can meet them with your Union Rep and tell them your side of the story. Mack is going to have a hard time finding anyone who will believe at sixteen you were helping your father plan and start fires," Captain Clarke said.

"Captain Rouke is probably going to be an issue though," Hawke commented.

Captain Bastian Rouke was the Captain for Second Shift here at the Twenty-First house. I didn't know he had lost his son in one of the fires that my father started. I had discovered that after I got here, and so far, I had been lucky enough not to come across him on my shifts. I knew he wouldn't recognize me. He had never seen me before, and my face had never been in any of the newspapers about my father. Still, there was a small fear inside me that he would know who I was just by looking at me. I knew if he discovered who I was that it could be a problem. Even though I wasn't the reason his son was dead, I was still the son to the man who was that very reason. He might not handle it well and it would be best for me to not be alone with him until I knew for certain how he would feel toward me.

"I will speak with him. It would be best for him to discover this piece of information from a friend as opposed to the grapevine. It will be hard for him to hear, but he will come to see and understand that Cyrus is not his father and cannot, *should not*, be held accountable for his actions. Just like the rest of us are not to be held accountable for the actions of our parents," Captain

Clarke said, his eyes hard.

I would definitely be allowing him to speak to Captain Rouke on my behalf, but only because I felt like it would be best coming from a third party that Captain Rouke trusted. All I could do though, was hope that he would be able to handle the truth. I had to trust that he would be able to handle that I was working in the same house as him.

I knew we didn't work the same shift and the odds of me ever working under him were slim, but even being in the same firehouse as him could be a quandary. He was a superior and if he wanted to he could have me transferred to a different house. To a house that might have a serious problem with my DNA and with me being gay. It wasn't a situation I wanted to be in, but it was out of my hands. All I could do was hope that things would work out and that Investigator Mack would find someone else to play around with.

Our conversation was cut short by the alarm going off. The shift was just starting and with some luck, things would go well today. If I was really lucky, maybe tonight I would be able to see Damon again.

CHAPTER ELEVEN

Damon

THE SECOND I walked into my office, I noticed the brown envelope sitting on my desk. It hadn't been there when I left last night and considering it was just after nine in the morning, there was only one thing that could be in that envelope. Something bad. It was either going to be from the Upper Brass or it was going to be from Taye's lawyer trying to get me to testify in Taye's defense. Both of which had to power to put me in a shitty mood for the rest of the day.

I had been in a half-decent mood this morning. Last night with Cy had been amazing and I was enjoying the time I was getting to spend with him. I had no idea where our relationship would go and I had learned long ago to not try and put a label on anything, or a clock. It was better to let life take its course and see how it would all play out naturally. Still, I was hoping to be able to see him again in a few days. When I was with him I didn't feel like a Captain or the older brother of the serial arsonist. I was just myself. I could be just myself and not have to worry about how I felt or what I did. I could be me and I desperately needed that in my life.

I knew the clock was ticking on my behavior. I couldn't keep acting the way that I was. I couldn't keep drinking and using drugs. I had to get my life back on track. I had to smarten up, be responsible, and get back to who I was. I knew it wasn't going to be easy, but it was something I had to do or I risked my career and that was something I couldn't stand for.

I also knew that I could be risking my career by being with Cyrus. I should never have done it. The second I discovered he was a Probee, I should have ended things. I never should have slept with him again, much less multiple times since.

Even though I knew I could lose my job by being with Cy, I couldn't bring myself to stop seeing him. I didn't want to lose my career, it was all I had, but I also didn't want to stop seeing Cy. Being with him made me feel so good and not just in a sexual manner. He made me feel like I used to feel before this whole mess started with Taye.

I felt alive around him.

When I was with him, I didn't want to drink or do drugs just to escape from the stress or horror of my life. I couldn't lose him, not right now. We would just have to be extra careful to ensure no one discovered about us just yet. Eventually, it could come out, but it would have to be after his probation period.

It wasn't just for me, but for him as well. He deserved the chance to make a name for himself, to build respect and a reputation as a firefighter without it being connected to his relationship to me. The last thing I wanted for Cy was for people to think he only made it because he was sleeping with a Captain. That wouldn't be fair to him and he didn't deserve to have that following him around.

Letting out a sigh, I closed my door and made my way over to my desk. I picked up the envelope and saw that there was no return address on it. I turned it over and opened it before pulling out the letter. I immediately knew that it wasn't from the Upper Brass by the lack of the Fire Department insignia at the top of the page. I was starting to think getting a letter from the Upper Brass would have been better than what I got, because what I got was a subpoena and a notice that Taye's court date had been moved up to next week.

Five days from now.

I collapsed down into my chair as I read the letter again. I thought I had a month before the trial to prepare myself for it. I thought I would have a month for Barba to try and convince Taye to take a deal. Now I was only getting five days before I would have to be in court. And I would have to be there to testify against my own brother.

I knew Taye's lawyer was going to try and make me testify for Taye, to prove that our childhood was the cause for his actions, but it wasn't going to work for him. I couldn't understand why his lawyer would ever want me to testify, because I didn't turn to criminal activity to cope with our childhood. I wasn't an arsonist and nothing he had to say would ever change that Taye was born broken and hadn't been made broken by his childhood.

I reached for my cell phone and pulled it out of my pocket. I looked first to see if I had gotten any texts from anyone, mostly Cy, but there was nothing new. I then pulled up Barba's number and hit the call button.

I didn't even hesitate to call him at this hour. I knew he would have been awake already and going over casework. There was no way he didn't know that the trial had been moved up to five days. I could picture Barba now, sitting in his office freaking out as he tried to prepare for a trial that he was supposed to have another month to prepare for. He was also going to have to get ready to cross-examine me in court. We had both believed that I wouldn't have to testify and that Taye's lawyer truly wouldn't want me to testify for Taye. Now that had gone out the window and Barba was going to have to prepare for my cross. I highly doubted anything Taye's lawyer had to say would sway the jury, but you never knew how someone would vote. All Taye needed was one jury member to be on his side and he would be acquitted of all charges. We had to get all twelve on our side, and that in and of itself was stressful as hell.

"Barba," he barked into the phone as he picked it up, the stress very clear in his voice.

"I take it you got the news," I said, without introducing myself. I knew he would know me based on my voice.

"Fuck. Fox is hoping that he can catch us off guard by pushing the trial date up. He wants us to miss something or screw something up so he can twist it all around to get Taye off. It's not going to work. I will be ready for the trial. No matter what."

I could hear how determined he was and that was something about Barba, he thrived under pressure. He wouldn't let this throw him off, it was going to do the opposite, and Taye's lawyer was not going to be prepared for the storm that was coming his way.

"I got a subpoena to testify for Taye. It looks like Fox is going to try and use our childhood to get him off."

"It's the only play he has to make. Taye has been through psychological evaluations and nothing came back that would work to get him off on non-compos mentis. He has to attack his childhood and he will have a Shrink that will back him up. It's a smart move, because there isn't anything that could say definitively that his childhood didn't alter his mind. Even when I prove that your childhood didn't turn you into an arsonist, a Shrink could counter that everyone's mind reacts differently to childhood trauma. It's a Hail Mary and it's not going to work, I don't care what I have to do. His victims will be getting justice."

"What do you need me to do?" I was more than willing to help out in any way that I could.

"Keep your head down and stay out of trouble. Anything could be used against us to justify Fox's defense. I need you to be completely honest with me, is there anything that Fox could have on you that would help with his defense?"

There was a loaded question. I highly doubted that Fox would have anything that could be used against me. I knew he could use my drinking, drug use, and promiscuity from the past few months, if he found out about them, but I highly doubted he had anything that would show my actions. I had been careful to keep everything that I had done completely discreet to ensure that no one discovered what I had been doing. My career could be in jeopardy if anyone discovered what I had been doing. With that said, I wasn't about to tell Barba about it. He didn't need more stress about the case and I wasn't in the mood for a lecture.

"No, there isn't anything. He could try and bring up how my parents were with us, but they weren't any different than millions of other parents in the world. He doesn't have anything."

I was confident on that. It would be insane for anyone to believe that our parents were to blame for Taye's actions. He had always been broken. Ever since I could remember, he had been different. There was nothing that our parents had done to make Taye that way. No, our father shouldn't have gotten him so involved in the Fire Department, but it wasn't like he knew this would be the result. Taye was just looking to lay the blame on people who couldn't defend themselves and I wasn't going to allow it. He deserved to be in prison for the rest of his life, it was just that simple.

"Good. Keep it that way. I have to go, but I will reach out before the trial so we can prep."

"I'll make sure I'm available. I appreciate it, Barba."

"I'll be in touch," Barba said, before he ended the call.

I gently tossed my cell phone down to my desk as I let out a sigh. This whole mess was turning into a circus and I really wasn't in the mood for it, but I was going to have to find the strength to get me through it. If I had to get up onto the stand and talk about my childhood, then I would do it, because Taye's victims deserve to get justice.

Tristan deserved to have justice.

I couldn't let my mind focus on all of that right now though. I had a shit load of paperwork to get through and I still had Mack to deal with. I would be speaking with him today about Cy. I wasn't going to tolerate him attacking Cy. He had handled his father's case wrong. He never should have interrogated Cy or kept him in a holding cell with grown ass adults. He put his life in danger by doing so and there was no excuse for it. I was going to be squashing that shit today before it went to the next level.

***

It was just after eleven in the morning when there was a knock at my door. I knew it was going to be Mack. I had reached out to him and told him to come in right away. I thought he would be here an hour or so ago, but apparently he decided to take his sweet ass time to come in. That was something else with Mack, he had been here for so long he forgot that he wasn't in charge, he wasn't a superior to anyone. He had experience over most of the other investigators, yes, but that meant nothing when it came to rank. He was getting to be more loose with the chain of command and that was also something he needed to be corrected on.

"Enter," I called out, and I started to gather some of the papers that were all over my desk and get them in order. He didn't need to see what I was working on.

The door opened and Mack walked in, closed the door, and then plopped down in one of the chairs across from me. It added to my annoyance that he felt like he didn't need to stand and show respect while waiting for permission to sit, like he was supposed to do. Most days, I would have let it go, but not today. Today, it was time for Mack to learn his place once again, and if he didn't like it, then he could finally quit and I would be free of him. I knew Barba would be all too happy to get rid of him working cases.

"I didn't give you permission to sit. This isn't your office and you will not treat it as such, nor disrespect me," I started with a clear edge to my voice as I sat up straight.

"Sorry, I didn't mean any disrespect, Sir," Mack said as he slowly stood up. I could tell he wasn't happy, but I didn't give a damn. I outranked him and he was going to have to suck it the fuck up.

"It has been brought to my attention

that you have an issue with Probee MacMillan."

"I investigated him when he was sixteen. His father is Jamie McDougal, and I had a strong feeling that he was helping his father to plan the fires and help him start them."

"I read the file and your investigation into him. Your so-called *feeling* resulted in you arresting a sixteen year old who just lost his mother. You kept him in an interrogation room for twenty-eight hours, no food, no water, no bathroom breaks, no child advocate, nothing that followed his rights. Then you placed him in an adult holding cell for the remainder of the forty-eight hours without food and water and had adult criminals in there with him. Once again violating his rights. And you did all of that on a feeling. Does that sum it up?" I asked in a growl.

"It's more complicated than that, Sir," Mack said with a tightness to his voice.

"It's more complicated than you violating a sixteen year old boy's rights? Because from where I'm sitting it looks like you had a vendetta against him and were looking to use him to make a bigger name for yourself. *You violated his rights.* You went against multiple protocols and now you are trying to ruin his career. I'm going to need you to give me a really good reason why I shouldn't suspend you pending an investigation."

Oh, I had heard all about Mack's visit to Station House Twenty-One this morning. He was down there talking shit about Cy when he was supposed to be in my office speaking with me, like I had ordered him.

"He was involved, Sir. I *know* he was involved. He shouldn't be a firefighter. We already have one firefighter up on arson and murder charges, we don't need to create another arsonist, another black spot to this department. People need to be aware that he lied on his application and of his connection to one of the most deadliest arsonists that the State has seen."

"All I'm hearing is that you have a vendetta against him. You had no proof, because there is none. He was a sixteen year old kid. He didn't know his father was an arsonist. He didn't help plan anything outside of a school dance. You are blinded, I don't know why, but you are blinded by his family, and I'm done. He didn't have to report his connection to McDougal to the Upper Brass. He only has to report on his own criminal background, which he doesn't have. What you have done, it is unacceptable, both past and present. You are officially suspended, pending an investigation."

"You can't do that," Mack instantly said, jumping to his feet, and I could hear the barely controlled rage in his voice.

"I most certainly can suspend you and I have every right and grounds to do it. You violated a child's rights. You went against protocols. You could have compromised that case's integrity if McDougal's lawyer had gotten wind of what you had done. And this isn't the first time you've compromised a case with your lack of professionalism. You're suspended and I honestly don't know if you will ever be allowed back. Clear out your desk. I will be in contact with your F.O.P Rep and they will let you know how the investigation is going."

I was done with Mack. I had more than enough proof to show that his competence in his work had been decreasing and it was time for him to retire. I also had multiple people who would be willing to vouch that Mack needed to be put out to pasture. It was time, and how he'd handled McDougal's case was more than enough proof. Fuck, Cy could still sue the department for his actions if he wanted and he would win. Mack was putting us all in a difficult and vulnerable position and I was not going to tolerate it any longer. It was time for a change and the Upper Brass were just going to have to jump on the bandwagon with this one.

Mack gave me one very dirty look, but he didn't comment, before he turned and headed out. I knew it was going to be a long process with him. I highly doubted he was going to take retirement with grace, but he would see soon enough that he had no choice but to take retirement or he risked being disgraced and fired without his pension.

Once I was alone, another sigh escaped me and I couldn't help but think I was starting to sound old. Mack had been handled for now. Now it was time for me to turn my full attention to Taye's trial and with any luck, we would win and I could put that behind me as well.

CHAPTER TWELVE

Cyrus

TO SAY THE past few days had been shit wouldn't even come close to it. I knew that it would get around that my father was Jamie McDougal, but I had underestimated the power and speed of the gossip mill within the Fire Department. Within forty-eight hours everyone knew about my connection and everyone had an opinion about it. Most were nice enough to only talk about it behind my back. There were some though, who felt it was appropriate to tell me exactly what they thought right to my face and while on a call. Every time we pulled up to an accident scene or a fire and another company was there, I would get looks, there would be whispers, and then there would be the ones who came right up to me to inform me that I shouldn't be there and was a disgrace to the department.

I normally would ignore shit like that, but most of the guys would jump to my defense before I could even think about walking away and focusing on the job. It helped to know that all of the guys had my back. That no matter how rocky things might get, I was going to have a safe place with Station Twenty-One. That didn't change that today still fucking sucked.

Damon had texted me, asking if I wanted to come by tonight and I had quickly replied yes. The only light in my life right now, the only thing that was simple and just fun was my time with Damon. I knew it wouldn't always stay simple and fun, there was going to come a time when shit between us got real and problems would show up, but I didn't care, because right now it was fun and freeing. He always knew how to make me feel good and he always knew what I needed. It was as if our bodies had known each other for life times and they were enjoying reconnecting with each other.

I grabbed my coat from my locker and

made my way out of the firehouse. Most of the guys had already left for the night and I was the last one. I had decided to take a shower before heading out so I didn't smell like smoke. I knew Damon wouldn't care, he would be used to it, but I still didn't like the smell of smoke seeping from my skin where I could smell it all night.

I exited the building and just as I reached the parking lot I saw Captain Rouke making his way across the parking lot toward me.

Fuck.

I had yet to see the man, even before all this shit about my father came out. I had never met him and it wasn't because I had been avoiding him since I got there. I didn't even know that my father had killed his son. It was just because I was always gone before he arrived. This was not how I wanted to be meeting him for the first time and I had no idea what was going to happen. What he was going to say.

I knew Captain Clarke had spoken with him the day that Mack had shown up and spilled the beans about my father. Captain Clarke had pulled me aside the next day and told me that he had spoken with Captain Rouke and explained the situation. Apparently, Captain Rouke was upset, but he didn't appear to be upset with *me*. I was hoping that meant that he would be okay with me being in the same Station House.

"Probee MacMillan, a word," Captain Rouke said, once I was close enough to him.

"Aye, Captain," I said, because really

what else could I say.

"I wanted to speak with you for a moment and clear the air between us. I know we haven't met before, but I am aware that your father is Jamie McDougal. I want you to know that my son was killed in a fire your father started, but I suspect you are aware of that fact."

"Aye, I am now, Captain. I'm sorry about your son. I didn't know until Captain Clarke informed me."

That wasn't fully true, I'd learned about it from Damon first, but he didn't need to know that part.

"My son, he was just twenty-two when he was killed in that fire. He never got married or had children. He was my only child and he had a bright future ahead of him. He was very proud to be a firefighter and he was a natural at it."

I could hear the pain in his voice and I could see that it was a wound that would never scar over. Not that I would ever expect it to. To lose a child was bad enough, but he had lost a child to someone else's actions. Because my father had a compulsion that he couldn't control, Captain Rouke's son was dead.

I could feel the guilt building within me again and it made my chest ache.

I had tried to not feel guilty over the lives my father took and destroyed with his own actions, but it wasn't an easy thing. My mind naturally told me that I should have seen the signs. That I should have noticed what he was doing so I could have stopped it sooner. I knew logically that none of this was my fault. I was just a child and I had no training or knowledge to be able to see the signs of an arsonist. As far as I knew, my father was boring and as average as they come. Still, knowing something and believing it were two very different things.

"I really am sorry, Sir," I said. If I had been a bigger man, a better man, I would have told him I would transfer to another Station House, but I didn't. I didn't want to leave Twenty-One, it was the only place that I knew I would be safe to be myself. That wasn't something I wanted to lose.

"I'm not telling you this so you will feel guilty, son. I am telling you this so you understand that the firefighters your father killed, they were good men and I know they would be proud and honored that you have decided to become a firefighter."

I wasn't expecting his words, at all.

I was expecting for him to yell, demand that I leave, threaten me even. I definitely wasn't expecting to be complimented.

"Sir?" I managed to ask and thankfully, he understood what I meant, because I didn't know if I could get more words out at that moment.

"Every firefighter knows when they respond to a call that there is a chance they could die that day, but they run into burning buildings to save people anyway, because that's who we are. They died in the fires that your father started, but with you becoming a firefighter, they didn't die in vain. My son didn't die in vain, because now every life you save is a life they save with you. You have nothing to apologize for, Cyrus. You didn't start those fires, your father did. You didn't know what he was doing. You were a sixteen year old kid and if you were anything like my son at that age, you were too busy playing video games and talking about girls with your friends. Of course you didn't know what he was doing. Of course you didn't help, and of course you can't be held accountable for the actions of your father. Just like I would hope that no one held my son accountable for the questionable actions that I have made in my life." He flashed me a warm smile, before he moved closer to me and placed his hand on my shoulder as he continued.

"You could have buried your head in the sand. You could have left town and gone on to do something else. But you didn't. You enrolled into the Fire

Academy, you decided to become a firefighter, and that right there shows what type of man you are. I am honored and proud to share this fire house with you."

Well, shit.

If that didn't make a man misty-eyed, I didn't know what would. I didn't expect this to be happening. I thought he was going to lose his shit with me, but instead, he pulled some fatherly knowledge and got me all emotional. He understood. He got it without me having to explain or say a single word to him. He understood why I had to become a firefighter, why it was so important to me. He had every right to hate me and try to force me to leave, but instead he was welcoming me with open arms, and that cut deep.

"Thank you, Cap. It really means a lot to me. And I will do my best to honor your son's memory and every firefighter who lost their lives because of my father."

That was a promise that I could easily keep. I was going to make sure that I honored their memory and made them all proud. Captain Rouke was right, every life I saved was a life that they got to continue to live. When I go through those doors, I am doing it with all of them watching my back and hopefully, my fire brothers would help to protect me and keep me alive, so I could keep saving lives for all of us.

"I know you will do them all proud, that you will do *me* proud. Don't carry the guilt around though, Cyrus. It's too heavy and it's not your weight to carry.

That weight belongs on the shoulders of your father and only his. Stop making his job easier. He doesn't deserve it."

"I'll try," I promised. But I knew that promise was going to take some work to accomplish. I was just hoping that one day I would be able to achieve it.

"If you ever need to talk, I'm always here for you. Same as the guys on my shift. I have already explained the situation fully and they have your back. You don't have to worry about anyone in this house giving you any sort of problems."

"I truly appreciate that, Sir. And if I need to talk, I will reach out."

"Good. Now, go. Get out of here and have some fun. I have a desk full of paperwork waiting for me." He said it with a groan and I couldn't blame him.

The paperwork was insane and not something they talked about in the academy.

I gave him a nod and flashed a warm smile before he headed off. I made my way to my truck and climbed in. I sat there in the driver's seat for a moment, thinking over the conversation I'd just had with Captain Rouke. I was still shocked by his acceptance of the situation, by his lack of blame on me for my father's actions. I honestly had no idea how I was supposed to feel about it.

I felt a lot of things, but mostly just stunned. Never in a million years had I thought the conversation with Captain Rouke would go that way. I was very surprised but also very relieved that it had. I had to admire the fact that he was an understanding man and was able to separate me being my father's son and my father's actions as not being two side of the same coin like so many others did. I hated that he'd had to bury his son because of my father, but it did bring closure and comfort to me to know that he didn't hate me for it.

A ding from my phone snapped me out of my thoughts and I picked it up to see a text from Damon

You on your way?

Just leaving now. Be there soon, Daddy.

I quickly texted him back before I dropped my phone into the cup holder. I knew he was waiting for me and I didn't want to keep him waiting any longer. My own excitement began to build, too.

Letting out a long, slow breath to calm myself down, I pushed my thoughts and feelings about my conversation with Captain Rouke away and focused on getting to Damon's place. I was going to be seeing him and I knew he would make all of my troubles melt away and right now, I needed that more than anything.

CHAPTER THIRTEEN

Damon

I WAS CONFIDENT that I was going to throw up at any minute. I was stuck in one of the stairwells within the courthouse as I waited for my turn to testify. It had been five days since I had been told that Taye's trial date was pushed up and today was the day I was set to testify in open court about our childhood. I knew Taye's lawyer was counting on me to tear my parents apart, but that wasn't going to happen. I wasn't going to let him get away with what he had done.

The past five days had been a rollercoaster. I was enjoying the time I got to spend with Cy. He was so easy to be around and there was a certain kind of peace when I was with him. We had seen each other three times in the past five days and each night was perfect and amazing.

I was becoming addicted to him and I knew it. Not just to his body, but to his personality and presence. He had a way of calming down the anxiety and stress inside me. A way to bring the peace to the storm within me.

I'd never expected to feel that way

about anyone, especially someone who was so much younger than me. I knew it was crazy and the chances of us lasting was so slim it was almost impossible, but even knowing that, I couldn't bring myself to stop seeing him.

I wanted him all the time.

Just seeing him and I had to fight with my cock to stay down. He was perfect, as if he was made for me and me alone. Our bodies fit perfectly together and I doubted I would ever get tired of having him around me.

The door to the stairwell opened and my stomach flipped thinking it was going to be the Bailiff to tell me it was my turn. I instantly relaxed when I saw it was Cy coming in. He had come today to provide me with some moral and emotional support. I knew people couldn't see us interacting with each other, at least not more than colleagues would, but I appreciated him being here with me. Just knowing that I would be able to look out into that courtroom and see him sitting there was enough to allow me to breathe again.

He flashed me a warm smile as he closed the door. He was dressed in an all black suit and he looked very good. If we weren't in a courthouse, I would have been tempted to press him up against the wall and fuck him right here.

"How are you holding up?" Cy asked, gently.

I had told him last night that I was worried about testifying. It had been years since I had to testify in court for a case and never for my own flesh and blood.

"I feel like I am going to throw up. This isn't a position I ever expected to be in. Even after Taye was arrested I didn't think I would have to testify. I wasn't even planning on attending the trial, let along being in it. How is it going?"

Because I had to testify, I couldn't be in the courtroom until I had testified. It was standard procedure to ensure that a witness wasn't influenced by what either lawyer said or things other witnesses might disclose. I was stuck here in purgatory until it was finally my turn.

"I have no idea. This is my first time in court. I didn't even go to my father's trial. The jury members, they have no expression on their faces. I can't get a read on 'em. Barba doesn't look worried, though, and it sounds like a solid case."

"What about Tristan, did he testify

yet?"

"Aye, he did really good. He didn't shake at all when Fox was questioning him. There are a lot of firefighters sitting behind Taye, showing their support to him. I don't know why, but I didn't expect that," Cy said, shaking his head as he sat down beside me on the stair.

I didn't surprise me at all that there would be firefighters here, most of which would be Taye's fake friends. The ones who needed him to be innocent so they could try and use their friendship with him to get ahead in their careers. There would also be an Upper Brass or two that would grapevine the information on the trial to others. Grown ass men and at the end of the day, we were nothing but a bunch of gossiping fourteen year old girls.

"They have to be here in case he is acquitted. They need to show support without showing the city that the Fire Department is supporting him. You have to remember this isn't just about arson cases or murder cases. This is a firefighter. A *legacy* firefighter. The Fire Department can be sued by every survivor and loved one who lost someone in a fire that Taye or Wilson started. If Taye loses, the Fire Department will be out hundreds of millions of dollars, which means the city will be out that amount. As horrible as his crimes are, the city is hoping he doesn't lose today because then any class action suit loses all hope of being granted."

"So the city would rather have someone as dangerous as Taye back on the street than pay people what they are owed?" he asked, disgust lacing his voice, and I knew that information was a shock to him.

He was new to all of it, but this wasn't my first rodeo with the city and payouts. We weren't talking about a couple of million, we were talking about easily a hundred million between all of the surviving victims and loved ones of those who didn't make it. It would be a nightmare for the city if Taye lost.

"It's a lot of money and you have to remember, Cy, that the city is run by politicians and they don't like giving up their money. He's not going to get away with it, everyone knows that, shit, even he has to know that, but that doesn't change that the Fire Department has to show some type of support for Taye."

"They won't let him back in though,

right? I mean, even if by some miracle he is able to get acquitted, the Fire Department won't just give him his job back, right?"

"It's not that simple. Legally, if he is cleared of all charges, he has every right to return to work. But, the Upper Brass can delay his return to work with a bunch of procedures that they would need to take to get him re-instated. They would also be looking for a way to force him to take very early retirement or to place him into a position that would force him to quit. Such as putting him in as a file clerk. Taye could also fight to get his position back with his union rep and a lawyer. He could easily argue he was wrongfully terminated. He could make it appear like Tristan had a vendetta against him and made up all of those lies. That he was there to try and get Wilson to turn himself in and Tristan misunderstood or some other bullshit."

"So, if he gets acquitted it would be a shit show," Cy simply stated, and I nodded. That summed up everything perfectly.

"It'll be fine, that's not going to happen. All the jury will need to see are the two dead kids and hear Tristan's testimony. That's all they need to convict him. The other fires might be circumstantial, but even if we only get a conviction on the homicide of Wilson and attempted homicide of Tristan and Detective West, Taye will go to jail for life."

That was the only reason I was so confident that we would get a conviction on Taye. Arson cases were hard to prove, even when you had a shitload of evidence. If the fire didn't destroy the evidence, the firefighters did when they put the fire out. But homicide and attempted homicide, that had real evidence. There were fibers, shell casings, witnesses, real evidence that ADA Barba could present to the jury and the jury could actually see it. We also had Tristan and Detective West who survived Taye trying to kill them. They were the perfect witnesses, trained to pay attention to even the smallest details and to be able to remember what happened to them with perfect recall. There was nothing that Taye's lawyer could do to discredit them.

The only hope that Taye had was if his lawyer could convince the jury that he couldn't be held accountable for his actions due to a mental deficiency. In this case, he was using our childhood as that defect. It wasn't going to work, because I wasn't going to allow it. It was time for Taye to finally take responsibility for his actions.

Before any more could be said between us, the door opened once again and a Bailiff stood on the other side. I knew without him even having to say anything that it was my turn. The court recess was over and it was showtime again.

"Captain Amaro, they are ready for you," the Bailiff droned in a calm voice, but I could hear the edge to his voice. He most likely wasn't too happy about Taye trying to kill a cop. Court officer or not, he was still law enforcement and he wouldn't be happy about someone trying to kill a fellow brother.

I gave a nod and both Cy and I stood up. I had him walk ahead of me, mostly so I could get a look at his ass one last time before I had to testify. It was a great ass and it looked amazing in the trousers he was wearing.

Fuck, I could not wait until this was over and I could fuck him.

I had planned to wait until we got back to my place, but now I was thinking about pulling off to some deserted area on the way home and pounding into him with him lying across the hood of my car. I had to quickly push that image to the side as I could feel my cock getting hard. The very last thing I needed was going into court with a raging hard cock for everyone to see.

As we approached the door, I let out a

long and slow breath, calming my nerves one last time before the door opened and I walked into the courtroom. It was as busy as I had expected it would be. The whole place was packed on both sides. I knew that the one side would be all cops, but there were also some firefighters here to show their support of Detective West and for Tristan.

Detective West may have begun the investigation into Taye and was planning on arresting him, but he had done it with good intentions and fellow firefighters had come around once they heard all of the evidence against Taye and what he was suspected of doing. It also helped to know that Tristan had witnessed Taye killing Wilson and tried to kill him. Going against the brotherhood was not easy, but they also defended and stood by their own even against a fellow brother once it was clear that one was in the right and one was in the wrong.

Cy left me as he went to go and take his seat next to Captain Clarke. His whole team was here to show support for their fellow brother and I appreciated it, but at the same time, I didn't like that others would be hearing about some of the things I'd had to deal with growing up. I didn't doubt for a single second that Taye hadn't told his lawyer about some of the more violent incidents within our home growing up. Just like I knew he would have left out him starting fires and killing animals when he was a child.

I made my way over to the stand and after being sworn in, I sat down and waited for the circus to start.

Fox, Taye's attorney, stood and spoke as he walked over to me. "Captain Amaro, you are the Defendant's younger brother, correct?"

"I am."

"And how would you describe your childhood?"

"It was fine, pretty average," I said with a small shrug. I wasn't going to be giving him anything until I saw what he had.

"Average? According to the Defendant, your father was a mean and violent drunk and your mother was checked out for the most part. Is that how you think everyone's childhood was like?" Fox asked, gently, but I knew it was a bullshit tone. He didn't care about hurting anyone's feelings. He just wanted to win and rake in the money.

"Was our mother checked out most of the time, yes. Did out father drink after work, yes. And yes, at times he got violent and he threw things or yelled. But he never raised a hand to either of us, same as my mother. Our father, as you know, was a firefighter and with that came some problems, but he was loving toward us. Taye had problems his whole life and none of them were because of our parents."

"You were not here to hear Dr. Hamilton's testimony, but after doing a deep evaluation of your brother, it is his professional opinion that the neglect, emotional, and mental abuse has caused irrevocable damage to your brother's mind. You yourself are also seeing a therapist, a Dr. Raitt," Fox started, but Barba cut him off.

"Objection Your Honor. The Defense has no access to the witness' medical file."

"Your Honor, it goes to the Defendant's defense that their childhood has caused irrevocable damage, and therefore, he cannot be held accountable for his actions. The witness' mental stability is completely within the realm of questioning," Fox easily countered and I knew he was going to win. It was fine though, because I was seeing a Shrink *because* of Taye's actions.

"Overruled," the Judge snapped.

"Answer the question, Captain Amaro," Fox said, his voice laced with a smug tone that made me want to punch him.

"After Taye's arrest and him trying to kill one of my subordinates, the Upper

Brass in the Department felt it would be best for me to speak with the departmental Shrink to express my feelings and thoughts on the matter. I am still on full active duty. I am not medicated or being requested to take time off. It's just procedure," I simply said in a calm voice.

"*Allegedly* tried to kill Investigator Cole," Fox corrected.

"You can't really claim it's *alleged* when the person he tried to kill still lives," I easily countered.

"Your commentary is not needed, Captain Amaro. Stick to just answering the questions," Fox said and it was clear he wasn't pleased with my comment.

I simply gave him a shrug before he turned and picked up a piece of paper from the table. "It is your claim that you have no mental demons from your childhood?

"That is correct."

He spoke as he turned the paper around to reveal a photo. "Then how do you explain your homosexuality, Captain?"

My blood ran cold as I saw the photo. It was of me and another man kissing outside of the hotel room that I frequently rented. I had no idea that they would be going to hotels and getting security footage.

How the fuck did he even get the warrant for the footage?

And how would he have known to look for it?

He must have had someone following me and I didn't notice. Taye didn't know I was gay. I had kept it hidden my whole life from everyone in my family. I could hear the whispers within the courtroom. This was a shock to everyone and I had no idea how I was going to explain this.

"Objection, Your Honor, the witness' sexual orientation has nothing to do with this case," Barba said, as he popped right up.

"I have to tell you, Counselor, I am agreeing with ADA Barba. You better have a good reason for this display," the Judge said to Fox.

"The witness has claimed that his childhood hasn't left any negative marks on who he is as a man today. This photo is just one of many that would suggest he is lying," Fox said.

"Last time I checked, sexual orientation wasn't a mental defect," Barba countered.

"Some would argue it is. Dr. Hamilton is fully prepared to retake the stand to speak on how some children, especially males, who grow up in a violent and abusive home will turn to homosexuality in order to escape the abuse," Fox argued.

"Not in the eyes of the law," Barba said, annoyed by Fox and what he was trying to pull.

I was still trying to figure out how to breathe. This wasn't what I was expecting and I had no idea what I was going to say. How could I deny it, when he had a photo of me, apparently multiple photos of me.

But could I really say I was gay right here in this courtroom, in front of people that barely knew me?

"And under the law, I have the right

to question a witness about his career, personality, sexual orientation, and any addiction if it could be relevant to the Defendant's case, which this is. It has already been proven within the law that a person's sexual orientation can be altered from traumatic experiences," Fox stated.

The Judge took a breath and I could see that he was debating. It was a fine line and he wasn't sure how to walk it. After a moment he spoke. "I am going to allow this, but tread very lightly, Counselor," the Judge warned.

"Captain Amaro, that is you in the photo, correct?" Fox asked as he brought it over to me.

I could see that it was one of the random men I had hooked up with off Grinder. I didn't even remember his name. I knew what he wanted me to say, I knew what I had to say, I just didn't know if I could say it.

I looked out and saw Cy looking back at me. He flashed me a warm smile and gave a small nod. I could feel his support being sent to me. I moved my gaze over to Will, my best friend and a gay Captain within the Fire Department.

"It's okay," he mouthed at me before he gave me a strong smile.

I knew there was going to be a conversation about the news with him later. He was going to understand why I kept it quiet with everyone else, but he was going to be upset that I didn't tell him. He was gay and had come out himself not that long ago, so he knew what this felt like. Well, not like this exactly, but he knew how it felt to come out at our age. I never thought I would come out, but Fox was giving me no other choice.

Letting out a small sigh, I made sure I sat up straight and held my head up high. If I was going to be coming out about my sexuality, then I was going to be confident about it. I had nothing to be ashamed of.

"Yes, that is me in the photo. And to answer your next question, yes, I am gay."

Holy fuck.

That actually felt good.

CHAPTER FOURTEEN

Cyrus

MY HEART SANK as I could do nothing but sit there and listen to Taye's lawyer trying to force Damon to admit to being gay. It disgusted me to begin with that he was trying to use Damon's sexuality as a way to justify Taye's defense. Being gay had nothing to do with a mental deficiency and it wasn't an excuse to justify starting fires and killing people. I wanted to scream at Fox to shut the fuck up and leave Damon alone, but I couldn't. I couldn't do anything but sit there and watch while Damon fought with his thoughts and emotions.

"Yes, that is me in the photo. And to answer your next question, yes, I am gay," Damon said with pure confidence.

I couldn't help the smile that spread across my face. Damon had been forced to come out of the closet, but he was doing it with grace and confidence and I was very proud of him. I could see Captain Clarke giving Damon a warm smile and I knew that the Captain was very proud of his best friend. I also knew there was going to be one hell of a conversation between them later.

"I have a lot of photos, over fifty of

them, with you and different men, some of the photos are you with multiple men going into a hotel room. Some of the photos show the men carrying alcohol and drugs. You can clearly see that there are ecstasy pills and cocaine in at least a dozen photos. Have you ever done drugs, Captain?"

I knew that Damon had been with other men—shit, we met on Grinder—but the drugs were new. I didn't know he had been with other men who were drug users or that he might have done some. I wasn't a prude. I wasn't a stranger to party drugs. I had never partaken in them, but I had been to a few parties where they were being passed around. I didn't expect for Damon to be the type of person to be using drugs, so that accusation came way out of left field.

"Within the past three months I have done ecstasy and cocaine on multiple occasions, but always while I am off duty."

"So, to clarify, promiscuous sexual activity, drug use, and drinking. It sounds to me like your childhood left its own scars on you, Captain," Fox said with a smirk before he continued. "No further questions, Your Honor."

Fox went back over to his seat as Barba stood up and I was really hoping he was ready to do damage control, because there was no way he saw any of this coming.

"Captain, let's get the giant elephant out of the room first, shall we? When was the first time you did drugs?" Barba started.

"Three months ago. I've never done

any drugs, not even marijuana, before that. I used to drink only on Friday or Saturday nights, and even then it didn't happen often. I also never used to have random hook ups. It all changed three months ago."

My heart went out to him. He had everything figured out and then three months ago his older brother went off the deep end and tried to kill someone he worked with. He discovered that his own brother was an arsonist who could give my own father a good run for his money. I still remember how I felt when the rug got pulled out from under me when I was sixteen. I didn't handle it well either, so I could understand Damon's need for an escape, in any form that he could get it in.

"What prompted the change in you?"

Barba asked gently.

"Taye's arrest. I felt guilty. I still feel guilty about not seeing it. Two innocent children were killed, a good Detective was almost killed, and one of my best investigators was almost killed. I just needed to not feel the guilt or anger for a little while. I admit, it was wrong of me to do it. It's not who I am, nor who I wish to be."

I could hear the guilt and remorse in his tone. I knew that Damon had been struggling with Taye's case and everything that it meant for him. I hated that I couldn't hug him right now and tell him it would be okay. I wished I could make it all better for him, but I was going to have to wait until we left to make that possible.

"What were your parents like?" Barba

asked.

Damon let out a small huff before he spoke. "Our mother was a good woman. She was great with us growing up until Taye was about twelve. Then, she started to feel overwhelmed with everything. Our father had been going through some hard fires, he lost a few men and he almost died three times. She was overwhelmed with having to be there for our father and his trauma. Our father, he never used to drink, but as the fires got worse, he started to drink more. He used to yell and throw things, but like I said, he never raised a hand to any of us. On his days off though, he would spend the time with Taye. They would go to the firehouse and use the burn house to run drills. Our father taught Taye how to start a fire and to control it."

God, I couldn't imagine why a parent would think that would be a good idea. I get that he was a firefighter and he wanted to share his job, something that took up the majority of his time with his children, but that didn't sound like good parenting to me.

"And what was Taye like?" Barba asked next.

"Objection, Your Honor, the witness is not a professional. He can't speak on my client's behavior," Fox tried.

"He doesn't have to be a professional to speak on his own memories. He grew up with the Defendant. He can speak on his own memories of his brother," Barba said, annoyed that Fox would even try and block his line of questioning.

"Agreed. The objection is overruled. The witness may answer the question," the Judge decided.

Nice try, Fox.

"He had always been different. There had been a few times where I overheard our parents talking about him. Our mother was worried about Taye spending so much time with our father at the firehouse. He had been starting fires since he was six. That's what made our father bring him around the firehouse. He thought Taye was just interested in what he did. It helped to control his urges for a bit, but then he began to start fires on his own, bigger ones. He had been killing small animals. One day when he was fifteen, I came home from school and he had taken our neighbor's cat, put it in a storage bin and set it on fire. He watched as it burned to death. I told our parents and

Taye had to go and speak with someone. After that, our father's drinking got worse and I wasn't allowed to be left alone with Taye. I would sleep in the couch in the living room so I wouldn't be alone in the bedroom at night with him."

Fuck all mighty, how the hell did Taye ever pass the mental evaluation for the Fire Department?

There were so many red flags and everyone seemed to ignore them because of his last name. He never should have been allowed to be in the Department. Yes, even if he hadn't been allowed to be a firefighter, he still would have been an arsonist, but maybe he would have been caught sooner.

"I'm sorry you had to see that, Captain. In your opinion only, do you think your brother knew what he was doing when he started those fires? When he tried to kill Investigator Cole and Detective West?"

"He knew. From a professional viewpoint, those fires were meticulously planned. Each home was chosen and surveillance was done. The smoke detectors were removed; the cameras were installed and hidden. For a decade, Taye had been able to plan those fires all the while working for the Fire Department. He was able to balance both lives without anyone even suspecting it. In my opinion, Taye doesn't have a mental deficiency. In fact, he's a criminal genius to be able to live in both worlds so perfectly."

Wasn't that the truth right there. No one suspected that Taye was an arsonist. Having to hide a huge part of yourself like that, it couldn't be done by someone who wasn't playing with a full deck. He was a genius and it wouldn't surprise me at all if he was a psychopath.

"Thank you, Captain Amaro. No further questions, Your Honor," Barba said with a polite smile before he turned and went back to his spot.

"The witness is dismissed. We will recess for ten minutes as the next witness is brought in," the Judge said, before he banged his gavel.

I watched as Damon got up and started to make his way toward me. He was heading for the door and I was not surprised at all when he kept going. I knew he needed air. That had been a lot and he had expected none of it. There was simply no preparing for that.

CYRUS

I made my way out after him and when I reached him I simply walked beside him, allowing him to guide the way. We headed out of the courthouse and he walked until we got to his vehicle. I didn't even think twice about climbing into the passenger seat as he got into the driver's side.

He turned the key in the ignition as he let out an audible sigh. He shifted the vehicle into gear without a word and then we were heading out of the parking lot.

I sat there in silence, knowing he needed some time to get his thoughts and feelings in order. The fact that he didn't tell me to go away indicated that he wanted me to be around him. That he wanted to talk about what I had just learned about him. I was more than happy to talk about it, once he was ready.

We drove to the waterfront and once there, he parked and climbed out of the car. I climbed out after him, making my way around to the front of the car at the same time he did. We walked down to the water and he sat down on top of one of the picnic tables. I climbed up beside him and just enjoyed the heat of the sun against my face for a beat.

"I'm sorry you had to find out that way," Damon started after a few moments of silence.

"You don't owe me an apology, D. We've only known each other less than a month. We're still learning plenty about each other. There's a lot you don't know about me, too. After everything you've been through with your brother's case, it's only natural that you would be looking for an escape from reality for a little while. What is going to happen when it gets back to the Upper Brass?"

I was worried that he might be losing his career all so he could make sure Taye was in prison where he belonged. That wouldn't be fair to him and it wasn't like he was a drug addict or in active field duty. He sat behind a desk all day. I was hoping that meant he wouldn't be fired.

"Random drug testing and I will be seeing Dr. Raitt for a lot more than I would like, but maybe it's a good thing. Be able to talk about all of this with someone that is a professional and can help me deal with the guilt in a healthier manner. I didn't want to say anything in court, but growing up wasn't peachy.

There are moments that still bother me. Some memories from Taye, but also my father and the pressure he put on me, the times where he just barely controlled himself from hitting me. Maybe it's time that I finally fixed my head."

I hated that he had been through something that still lingered inside him. I could understand what he was feeling, though. My life had been pretty perfect up until my father was arrested. After that, it went to shit for two years and I did some things I shouldn't have. Like having sex with my teacher and older men before I was even of legal age. Him speaking with a Shrink, it would be good for him. It would be a way that he could talk about what has been bothering him and he could get some tips on how to cope and work through it. And I was very relieved to hear that he wouldn't lose his job over it. He didn't deserve that.

"I think that's a great idea. If you feel like it could help, then you should do it and I completely support you. I know I'm not a professional, but I'll always be there if you ever feel like you need to talk about something," I said, flashing him a warm smile.

"I appreciate that. You need to know that even though I just came out, and by tomorrow everyone in the department will know I'm gay, it doesn't mean people can know about us. And that has nothing to do with me being ashamed or trying to put a genie back in a bottle. You're on probation and the last thing you or your career needs is people thinking you passed your probation period because you're sleeping with me. You need to establish a reputation and respect within the department before we drop that bomb into the water."

I was actually really relieved to hear him say that. I didn't want to hide our relationship, but I also didn't want it to come out just yet. I completely agreed with him. I needed to be able to build a reputation off of my skills and not because people thought I was that good at sucking cock. I was that good, of course, but it wasn't what I wanted people to talk about. I was also still dealing with the fallout of practically everyone knowing I was Jamie McDougal's son. I had to let the waters calm back down before something else came out.

"Aye, I completely agree. It actually

makes me happy to hear that you think that as well. I was worried you would be upset that I wanted to keep this, us, a secret for a bit longer."

"Not at all. Besides, sneaking around can be a lot of fun," he said with a sexy smirk and it had my cock pulsing. This man was sex on a stick and just as deadly.

"Aye, that it can. We headin' back to the courthouse?"

Fuck, I hope not.

"I wasn't planning on it. I had other ideas on how to spend the rest of the day," he said, flashing me a cheshire grin as he looked me up and down and I knew exactly what he was thinking.

"I was really hoping you would say that. I'm wearing the new toy you got me," I said, flashing him with what I hoped was a sultry smile.

Damon gave a groan before he stood up. "We have to go," he said in a hurried tone and I couldn't help but chuckle at the reaction.

We practically ran back to his car and climbed in. I buckled up mere seconds before he cranked the engine and reversed out of the lot. His excitement was damn near palpable, and quite contagious.

I knew everything between us was still so fresh and it would most likely simmer down, but until that happened I was going to enjoy every single second that I could with him.

EPILOGUE

Three Months Later...

Damon

IT WAS CRAZY what a difference three months could make.

Six months ago, my brother was being arrested for multiple arson and murder charges. My whole world had been destroyed and I spiraled almost out of control. For three months after that, I spent my time when I wasn't working fucking every guy that I wanted, getting drunk, and even doing drugs. Then just three months ago, Cy walked into my life and everything since has changed.

The pain, the anger, the guilt, the storm that had been raging inside of me started to disappear.

I was able to find my way back to myself and it was all because of him. The trial for Taye had been hard. Everyone discovered that I was not only gay, but I had been using drugs recreationally and screwing random men. It resulted in a very long conversation with Will, but I'd expected that. It also resulted in me being pulled into my boss' office first thing in the morning to discuss my future with the Fire Department. It wasn't anything extreme; it was exactly what I had expected. Random drug testing and mandatory therapy sessions with Dr. Raitt for the next six months.

I was fine with it and I was enjoying the therapy sessions with Dr. Raitt. He was helping me to resolve my guilt over Taye's actions. He was helping me to accept who I am and how to deal with some of the things that happened growing up. It had been good to speak to someone where I didn't have to worry about him judging me or trying to bring up things and throw them in my face later. I could tell him anything and he would listen and offer his thoughts or he would help to come to a realization on my own.

I had told him about Cy roughly a month ago and it had been very good to be able to talk about it with someone. I hadn't even been able to tell Will about him because he was Cy's Captain and I didn't want to make things awkward or weird for either of them, especially Cy.

He had also been doing really good for himself at the firehouse. He was building a reputation and I couldn't be more proud of him. Things were finally starting to cool off with him and other firefighters. He was finally making progress with all of that. It terrified the hell out of me knowing that he was running into burning buildings every day, but it was also something I was working through. The very last thing I wanted was to become my father or my mother. I had to be able to handle Cy being an active firefighter or our relationship was going to be doomed like theirs had been.

CYRUS

As for Taye, he was currently serving three consecutive life sentences in a maximum federal prison. He had been found guilty on all charges, including the arson cases. The only reason he didn't get the death penalty was because his surviving victims got together and decided that being trapped in prison for the rest of his natural life was a worse punishment then getting to go to sleep.

I have to say, I agree with them. At least while he is in prison, he will know what it feels like to be trapped in a place that you want nothing more than to escape from. As his brother, I should be horrified at the idea of him being trapped there, but knowing that he can't ever hurt another innocent person again is a huge relief.

I hadn't visited him and I have no

plans to. I knew he would never give me a straight answer about anything and I would just be feeding into his control. I was done with him having the control and trying to manipulate me into doing his bidding. It was time I got to live my life the way I wanted to live it, and that was exactly what I was doing.

I glanced over and saw Cy wiggle once again in his seat. We were currently heading to a restaurant in a nearby town. It was something we had started doing three months ago so we could have normal date nights and not have to worry about someone seeing us together. It was a compromise that we had come to.

We both knew we had to keep our relationship a secret for now. Cy deserved the time to build his skills and his reputation before we made our relationship public. However, we both wanted to try actual dating with each other and that meant going on real dates and not just fucking each other at one of our places. Going to a nearby town was the best solution that we could come up with. It would allow us to hold hands and kiss in public without having to worry about being recognized.

Tonight was date night and I was taking us to an Italian restaurant for dinner. Tonight was a bit different though, because tonight I had made sure that Cy wore tight pants, but also a vibrating dildo was currently in his ass to keep him nice and hard for me. To top it all off, there was nothing to stop him from coming except his own willpower. He was currently trying to handle the dildo on the middle setting and I could tell it was driving him crazy, but that was exactly what I wanted. I wanted his body so sensitive tonight when I fucked him that he couldn't stop screaming and begging for more.

"You okay there, Baby?" I asked, flashing him a smirk.

"Oh fuck, Daddy," he half moaned and whined.

I knew it was going to be a first for him and it was going to be difficult for him to get used to, but I knew he would love it and I was going to love watching him try to eat and have a conversation while he sat hard as a rock at the table in a room full of people for an hour or more.

The sex over the past three months had become very intense and remarkable. Cy was very open to try anything and his body was so responsive to me. It was as if we were both made for the other and only the other's body could bring true pleasure to each of us. There was a great deal of trust that went into what we had. He had to trust that I knew what his body wanted and would find pleasure in, and I had to trust that he would tell me when he needed me to slow down or stop. So far, we had been on the same wavelength and it felt amazing. I knew there was going to come a time when one of us had to say no or pump the brakes, but I was okay with that. It happened in every relationship and I would never push Cy to try something that I knew he wasn't ready for or something he wouldn't find pleasure in. What we were currently doing was new to him, but I knew he was going to love it because he had shown me that he would from our time together.

I pulled into the parking lot for the restaurant, and after turning my car off, I looked over at Cy. I could see the pleasure all over his face, but I could also see some nerves starting to build as well. I knew he had worn a plug in public, but this was taking things to the next level and I wasn't certain he was ready for it now that we were here. I reached over and placed my hand on his knee, making sure I had his attention before I spoke.

"Tonight can go one of two ways and how we spend it is completely up to you. The first way, I can turn the device off and we can go inside and have a nice dinner before heading back to my place. Or way number two, the device stays on and we go inside and have a nice dinner before going back to my place. I don't care what option we do. Both will result in a great night and us having amazing sex. The choice is completely up to you and what you are comfortable with."

I meant it, too. I didn't care what we did. All I cared about was getting to spend time with him. Being able to go out on a date like a normal couple. If the devices were on for it, then great, but if not then that didn't change how I felt. There would be no disappointment. I didn't want him doing something he didn't feel comfortable with, because then the fun was taken out of it and that wasn't the point in what we were doing.

I could see him thinking about it for a

moment, but after a second he gave me a warm smile. He moved in and pressed his lips against mine. I placed my hand on the side of his neck, pulling him into me and deepening the kiss.

I loved kissing him.

I usually didn't care for kissing much, but with Cy I could do it all day and night and never get tired of it. All too soon, he was pulling back and flashing me that sexy smirk of his before he spoke.

"Let's go."

Option two it was, and I would be lying if I said my own cock didn't get hard at hearing which one he had chosen.

We both got out of my truck and I placed my hand on the small of Cy's back, guiding him over to the entrance and inside. The place was pretty packed, not surprising considering I had to make a reservation just to get us a table. The hostess gave us a warm smile and I gave her my name for the reservation.

"Um... yes, right. Um, right this way," she said.

She guided us over to our table, which just so happened to be in the middle of the room. I guided Cy through the room and held his chair out for him. Cy slid into the seat and I sat across from him in my seat. I could see other patrons looking over at us and I could see a slight blush creep up Cy's cheeks, but I could also see the arousal in his eyes. He was enjoying this, just like I suspected he would.

"This place is nice," Cy managed to say as he looked around.

"It is nice. I've never been here, but everything that I read online said it was a great place with really good food. Do you have a favorite pasta dish?"

"Not really," he said with a small shrug.

He didn't even bother with looking at the menu; he knew I would order for him. It was something that we did. Cy was very easy going and he didn't mind being told what to wear or me ordering his food for him. He was pretty used to it from his past relationships and I liked that he trusted me with making these small decisions for him.

The waiter came over and I placed our drinks and food order. Once he left, I reached into my pocket and turned the device up a bit higher. Cy let out a whispered moan as the pleasure within him started to peak. I knew it wouldn't be long before he was coming for the first time tonight, the first of many.

"You okay?" I asked with a knowing smirk.

"Don't suppose we could just skip to dessert, huh?" Cy countered with a small smile as he tried not to wiggle too much in his chair.

"Now where would the fun be in that, Baby?" I said with a playful wink.

"How, um... how was work?" he asked, and I could tell he was trying to focus on a conversation and not the pleasure that was currently overtaking him.

"It was good. Busy with paperwork. We also have been going through Investigators. Ever since the Upper Brass discovered what Mack did to you on your father's case, all of the old timers have been getting looked over. The Upper Brass want me to go through their files and make sure they didn't compromise anyone's rights or take things too far. I have to go through their conviction rates as well. It would appear the Upper Brass are looking to tighten things up."

"That's not a bad thing, though."

It wasn't. It just meant I had a lot more work because even though the Upper Brass had finally figured out that some of the firefighters and investigators were too old school and they were getting lazy in their old age, not everyone wanted to retire. I understood that and there was no problem with having older people on staff. The problem came when they got too comfortable with their bad habits and laziness. Conviction rates were important and getting the right arsonist meant we would prevent future fires. It was time for the Investigation Division to get a complete overhaul and I was very happy with it finally happening.

"It's not. It just means more work for me, and some pissed off investigators, but they will simply have to deal with it. If they have done their job properly and to the best of their abilities, then they have nothing to worry about. What about you? How was your day?"

Things had gotten better for Cy with the other firefighters that he was frequently around outside of Twenty-One. There were still plenty of people who didn't believe he should be in the Fire Department but thankfully, they were fewer than they were three months ago when the news broke out about Cy's father. It also helped that people started to hear about how Mack treated him the night he arrested his father. That gained him some sympathy votes and even though I knew Cy wasn't happy about them, I was relieved to have less people to worry about.

"It was," Cy started, but then he stopped as he had to bite down on his lip to cover the moan that was threatening to escape.

I was still able to hear it though, and a quick look around told me the few tables around us could hear him. I kept my eyes locked onto him as he rode each wave as he came right there at the table. I knew his cum would be soaking into his boxers and then it would soak through his jeans and I couldn't wait until we left and everyone saw the wet spot on his pants.

Fuck, this man was perfect and one day, if everything worked out, I was going to marry him.

After a moment Cy let out a shaky breath as he tried to calm his body down, not something that was easy to do considering the device was still going.

"I'm sorry, I didn't quite get that, how was work?" I asked, flashing him a smirk.

"Um... it was, um, it was fine. We didn't have many calls today, so it was a good day in that sense."

"Good, I'm glad you had a good day. How's your night going?"

"Fucking awesome," Cy said with a shaky breath as the waiter brought over our drinks.

Once he left, I picked up my whiskey and held my glass up as I spoke. "Tonight is all about you, Baby. You came into my life a little bit over three months ago and you were only supposed to be a quick fling and that was all. But then you changed my whole world and now I can't imagine not having you in my life. You are a wonderful human being and I'm madly in love with you."

I could see the slight surprise flicker through his eyes. I hadn't told him I loved him yet, just like he had never said it to me, but we both knew the other felt it. We both knew we were in love, but we had no reason to say it with words.

Tonight, I was saying it and I had every intention of saying it every night after this.

"I love you, too," he said warmly as he

gave me the most radiant smile I had ever seen.

We clinked our glasses together and I knew that tonight was going to be the night that changed everything. He had already changed my world when I opened that hotel door to see him standing on the other side.

And he continued to change my world every day after that.

It had only been three months, but I was looking for thirty more years with him and I knew I would get it. Whether we were soul mates in another life or not, it didn't matter, because in this life he was my soul mate and I couldn't wait for whatever else the world had in store for us.

Thank you for reading Cyrus and Damon's story.
Continue the series with Jase, book 3 in Smokejumpers!

OTHER BOOKS BY EVIE

Federal Protection Agency

Mason

Rafe

Ryzen

Cooper

Noah

Damien

Sebastian

Gabe

Logan

Ruthless Empire

Courting Danger

Chasing Danger

Kissing Danger

Smokejumpers

Hawke

Cyrus

Jase

Gage

Jackson

Xavier

EVIE RILEY

Jasper Springs
Cade
Dawson
Drew
Grayson
Riley
Mitch

From The Edge
Shattered
Runaway
Jaded
Rescue
Hidden
Tormented

Gray Vale Pack
His Fated Mate
His Wounded Warrior
His Healing Heart

ABOUT THE AUTHOR

Evie Riley is a prolific, neurodivergent author known for her captivating MM romance novels. She has gained a significant following and topped the LGBT+ action and adventure bestseller charts with her series.

Evie's writing style often explores dark and gritty themes where her men must overcome difficult obstacles in their search for love, but she has also ventured into sweeter small-town romances, incorporating tropes like enemies-to-lovers, friends-to-lovers, age-gap, and forced proximity. She is known for crafting engaging romantic suspense novels and has a knack for creating interconnected series worlds that keep readers invested.

Interestingly, Ms. Riley has hinted at exploring new genres, such as Alien Omegaverse Romance, in the future.

Outside of writing, she enjoys spending time at the beach and has a quirky personality, described by her partner as ranging from cute to deadly, depending on her blood-chocolate levels.

Evie spends her nights writing bad boys in love, and her days wrangling the sweet boys she loves.

9 781773 576800